Books by Pamela F. Service

THE
RELUCTANT
GOD

THE RELUCTANT GOD

by Pamela F. Service

A JEAN KARL BOOK

ATHENEUM   1988   New York

Atheneum
Macmillan Publishing Company
866 Third Avenue, New York, NY 10022
Collier Macmillan Canada, Inc.

Text set by Haddon Craftsmen, Allentown, Pennsylvania
Printed and bound by Fairfield Graphics, Fairfield, Pennsylvania
Designed by Jean Krulis
First Edition

10 9 8 7 6 5 4 3 2 1

Library of Congress Cataloging-in-Publication Data

Service, Pamela F.
The reluctant god/by Pamela F. Service
p. cm.
SUMMARY: While his brother prepares to mount the throne of Egypt as the next member of the Twelfth Dynasty, the teenage prince Ameni is sealed in a secret tomb in a state of suspended animation, to be revived four thousand years later by the fourteen-year-old daughter of an archeologist.
ISBN 0-689-31404-3
[1. Space and time—Fiction. 2. Egypt—History—To 332 B.C.—Fiction.] I. Title.
PZ7.S4885Re 1988
[Fic]—dc19
87-16840 CIP AC

FOR SU

THE
RELUCTANT
GOD

PROLOGUE

England: Twentieth Century A.D.

Lorna's eyes were fixed on the window, but she didn't see the cold, rain-smeared school yard any more than she saw the history book open before her on the desk. Instead, she saw the golden sun-warmed cliffs of Egypt. Above them stretched clear unclouded blue. Below, threading a narrow belt of greenery, ran the river Nile. Under the cliffs she placed a village of low whitewashed houses, but her imagination left out the telephone poles and occasional TV antennas that usually sprouted about. Instead she put in an ancient-style temple, pennants flying, and pylons carved with monumental figures of gods and kings. For good measure, she threw in a luxurious royal barge sailing by and was just concentrating on the bejeweled figures on board when a shadow fell across her daydream.

She looked up into the scowling face of her history master. He did not bother with words; his expression said it all. She lowered her eyes to the textbook, resentfully forcing them to read about Parliament's squabbles with King Charles I.

All this was so boring, with edicts and insurrections and quarrels about the "divine right of kings." The ancient Egyptians would never have argued about that. Their kings had more than divine *right*. They were gods themselves, and nobody questioned it. She wondered if they really had been gods. But then, why not? Certainly if God wanted to work through other gods or even a man to get His message across, if He wanted to make a king a god in the eyes of his people, then surely He was powerful enough to do it. Wasn't their school chaplain always saying how God works in mysterious ways? Maybe this was one of them.

Feeling the history master scanning the class again, she dutifully turned a page, unsure what she had supposedly read on the last one. Her mind slipped back into Egyptian speculation. The aggravating thing was that they'd never know! She'd never be sure what it was like back then, how it was to live in a pharaoh's palace, or actually to be a mortal person and a god as well. They could read books, or dig in ancient ruins as her father did—and she did whenever she could—but they could still only speculate. They'd never really *know*.

Idly, she picked up a pencil and began doodling on the margin of her book. "Lorna" in ancient Egyptian hieroglyphics. The seated lion that stood for *L*; no *o* of course, because the Egyptians didn't bother with most vowels; then the oval mouth sign for *r*; the wiggly water sign that meant *n*; and finally the eagle for the concluding *a* sound—like the one that ended *Cleopatra.*

Fondly she looked at her doodling. How fine to have your name written like that on some grand stone monument for all eyes to see. Too many eyes had seen this one, she realized suddenly.

"Miss Padgett, I appreciate that this is a history lesson, but aren't you perhaps in the wrong century? Or, perhaps I should say, the wrong millennium?"

The girl next to Lorna sniggered. Ignoring her, Lorna grabbed for an eraser. "Sorry, Mr. Edwards." He was going on about defacing books, but she was thinking about the first part of his diatribe. Yes, she *was* in the wrong millennium. In the wrong country, too. A secret smile played about her lips. But she wouldn't be for long, not in the wrong country anyway. In a few weeks the term would end, and she'd leave all these boring people in their wet, cold England and rejoin her father in Egypt. And if she couldn't actually span the centuries, their work there would bring her as close to that as anything could.

The master's berating was running down. Lorna muttered appropriate abject apologies and turned her eyes back to Cromwell's Parliament. But already she was seeing again the cliffs and temples and the splendid royal barge where figures in jewels and fine linen robes gathered around a canopied throne and a true divine king.

5

ONE

Ameni's heart beat fast with excitement. True, this was a kid's game. But since he was playing it, he might as well enjoy it.

Hound and hares. At the moment, he and most of the others in the palace nursery were playing the hares. His youngest sister, Sithathor, was being the plump little hound.

Through the wooden sides of the linen chest, he listened to the distant excited voices. It sounded as if cousin Neferhent had let herself be caught, probably so she could help the little princess in her quest. Sithathor was yiping now like an excited hound following a scent.

They were several rooms away, giving him a chance to find a better hiding place. Lying in this heavy painted chest was sort of like lying in a coffin. He supposed that sort of thing was all right for tired old people—letting their bodies rest in a tomb while their souls lived in the afterworld with Osiris and the other gods. But he had too much living to do still. Tombs and such made him uneasy.

Cautiously Ameni raised the lid. Nobody about, not even a servant. Quietly he slipped out, taking deep, grateful breaths of fresh air. Then he looked about for another hiding place.

This was the birthing room. Unused at the moment, it waited for one or another of the royal wives to give birth. Near the door stood a shrine to Tawert, goddess of childbirth. Smiling mischievously, Ameni sprinted across the room, his sandals making only a breath of sound on the woven mats.

He bowed, gave a word of greeting to the goddess, and slipped in behind the statue. The bulk of the hippopotamus goddess would be good cover, and she shouldn't mind protecting him. Hadn't she presided at his birth? They said she had actually appeared to Queen Nofret, his mother, and comforted her against the sudden storm raging outside. Reportedly it had been a storm more violent than any remembered in the Nile Valley. Lightening and thunder had shaken sky and earth. Befitting, they said, for the birth of royal twins. Ameni's tutor, the priest Ankhrekhu, was fond of telling about it and how he had slipped the amulets over both infants' heads—a crystal one for him, a gold one for his twin brother Senusert, older by minutes and royal heir.

Ameni could hear his brother's laugh now; he must have

been caught by the eager little hound. The hunt would move this way soon. Time to find a new hiding place; it was against the rules, after all, to stay in one place too long.

Thanking the goddess, he slid from her protective shadow and cautiously flitted out of the room, down a hall and into the heat and bright sunshine of the nursery garden. He looked quickly about, then sprinted for a clump of papyrus growing beside the ornamental pool.

He rustled his way between the dry reeds and the outer wall of the pool. Above, the sky was bleached with heat, but here among the thin shifting shadows of papyrus, the richly colored tiles felt cool against his bare back. As he wriggled into a more comfortable position, the crystal amulet about his neck clinked against a deep blue tile.

Absently he looked down at the amulet, clear crystal carved into two fists clutching a dagger. Occasionally he and his twin exchanged amulets to confuse people. Of course, if the priests and royal advisors found out, they got furious, going on and on about how Senusert was to become king and Living God someday and his identity was nothing to be played with. Still, it was almost worth it to watch them go purple and launch into the predictable lecture.

Not that Ameni actually wanted to trade places with his brother. A king's training was arduous, and when the kingship finally came, it meant a life encased in duty. Every minute Senusert would be surrounded by courtiers and advisors, and there'd be endless religious duties and tedious processions and audiences, with the king having to sit under his heavy regalia as motionless as a stone god. Their father, Senusert II, was a strong king and cared for his people, but he was burdened with worries and responsibilities. Only on military forays, like his recent one into Nubia, did he really seem to enjoy himself as king.

The sun-flecked pool glinted before Ameni's eyes like the oceans in adventure tales. No, what he really wanted was freedom and adventure like Sinuhe, the story hero, who went off adventuring in distant Syria, or like the fabled ship-wrecked sailor who met the great bearded serpent of the Red Sea. What he'd like . . .

With a rustle and a triumphant cry, arms locked around his ribs, Ameni sprang forward, rolling onto the broad edge of the pool. After a moment's flailing, both combatants toppled into the shallow water.

Shaking drops from his short black hair, Ameni sat up in the water and looked at his giggling cousin. Neferhent's own black hair hid her face in a wet veil. The water still quaked around her as she laughed. "The hounds certainly caught you dreaming that time, hare."

Little Sithathor ran up to the pool edge, laughing and clapping her pudgy hands. "No, no, not a hare. He's a frog! Look, Ameni's a frog!"

"I am not!" he growled, standing up. He scissored his dripping arms before him like huge threatening jaws. "I am Sobek, mighty crocodile god, and I've come to eat bothersome little princesses."

Senusert and the other children had found the courtyard by now and laughed as Sithathor squealed in mock terror and fled towards the shadowy colonnade. She ran smack into the solid bulk of Merseger, the eldest royal daughter.

The bewigged, elaborately dressed girl looked primly down at her baby sister, whose plump brown body was naked except for a string of beads around her waist. Then with a glance at the twins and a smug smile, she turned and called down a hallway.

"Here they are. The two princes are here, playing like silly babies in the water."

"I am not playing in the water," Senusert objected, quickly sitting by the pool and splashing a sparkling handful of water at his twin. "Though I might be persuaded to."

"All right!" Ameni grabbed his brother around the knees and pulled him into the pool. Neferhent joined in the growing water war, until a deep authoritative voice cut through the noise.

"The tutors have been looking for the royal princes so long, I began to wonder what had happened to my brood." The pharaoh's tall figure stepped from the shadows, setting the jewels in his broad gold collar twinkling in the sunlight. The expression on the king's thin, lined face quavered between frown and smile. "But I see they have only become water serpents."

The three children bowed their heads to the pharaoh and clambered hastily out of the pool. The white linen of the boys' kilts and the girl's dress clung heavily to their bodies and dripped into dark spreading pools on the flagstones.

The king's laugh slipped into the hacking cough that had plagued him since returning from Nubia. He cleared his throat. "Well, since they are now water serpents, perhaps tutoring will do them no good. But then, maybe you two can do something with them."

He spoke over his shoulder, and two men joined him in the sunlight. General Renseneb, a short burly man, nodded brusquely at the dripping princes. "I believe, Prince Senusert, we had archery practice scheduled for this morning. Would you care to accompany me . . . eh, after changing into something drier?"

The older twin smiled sadly at his brother. "Well, if duty must call, I'd rather face my lessons today than Ameni's. Aren't you learning the names of the seven keepers and the seven watchmen and the seven heralds of the seven gates of the afterworld?"

Ameni only groaned and thumped his brother on the shoulder as the other went off with the general.

"Actually, your majesty, I had something else in mind for the prince today." A priest with shaven head and long white robes stepped up to the king. "Prince Amenemhat has already done a creditable if unenthusiastic job of learning the gates of the afterworld. Today it is to be another lesson in the language of the Hittites."

Ameni groaned again and said, "Venerable Ankhrekhu, you have already had me learn the languages of Syria, the desert dwellers, the Sea People, Punt, and Nubia. The land of the Hittites is so unimaginably distant, surely I needn't learn that as well."

Coughing, the pharaoh sat in a gilded chair a servant had silently brought up. "Ankhrekhu, since he was a baby, you've been teaching this boy more languages than I knew existed. I've never quite understood why, except that the god Osiris demands it. At least if my headstrong eldest son decides to take off and conquer the world, he'll have someone along to talk to the people that get in his way. But go along you two, and give me a few minutes to hide from my counselors and talk with the rest of this brood."

Immediately Sithathor plunked herself down in the king's lap and was joined by the children of various royal wives and finally by the nieces and nephews who shared the royal nursery. Merseger, looking prim, stood possessively behind her father's chair.

Ameni sighed and had turned to walk off with his tutor when Neferhent put a hand on his arm and whispered, "I hope you're better with Hittite than with hound and hares."

He scowled dramatically. "Hittites may be northern barbarians, but I bet they'd be more respectful than to dunk a king's son."

"Maybe, unless one is a king's niece." She laughed, then added, "Don't worry. If your father tells us any new tales from his Nubian adventures, I'll pass them on to you." She slipped away to join the others.

Ameni's smile soon dissolved into a sullen frown as he followed Ankhrekhu down the cool corridors of the palace. He'd been thinking how lucky he was not to be the royal heir. But he had as much tutoring as if he were, and on duller things at that.

For as long as he could remember, Ankhrekhu had been training him to be a priest of the god Osiris, Egypt's first king and now ruler of the otherworld. Ameni had dutifully learned the many rituals and chants as well as the names and forms of all the other gods in the great pantheon.

But in addition, Ankhrekhu insisted he be instructed in the languages of every major foreign people and learn too about their lands and odd customs. Ameni had gotten so that he absorbed new languages with comparative ease, though he imagined that was mostly from a desire to get it over with so he could linger on the more interesting parts of his schooling, such as use of the bow, spear, and throwing stick.

The two turned at last into the schoolroom. Sunlight slanting through the narrow windows danced with dust motes, and the warm air carried the familiar dry smell of papyrus rolls and sooty ink. The priest gestured for his pupil to sit, already so absorbed in thoughts of Hittite that he'd forgotten the state of the prince's clothes. Obediently Ameni sat cross-legged on the mat, but the day's heat had already dried the kilt to only a mild dampness.

Ankhrekhu opened a wooden chest and began clattering through a jumble of clay tablets. Ameni watched him with an odd affection. For all that he was a hard taskmaster, the priest was also a friend and, next to Senusert and Neferhent, his closest companion.

Ankhrekhu looked up at his pupil with his distinctive lopsided smile and handed him a tablet. "Now here's a letter in Hittite. Let's see how well you remember the symbols. Read it aloud for the sound first."

Ameni scowled at it. Bird tracks on a slab of mud. "Not only can these Hittites not write sensibly, their words are far too long to get the tongue around." Before his tutor could open his mouth, he added, "Yes, yes. Don't say it, I know. 'Different people, different ways.' I'll try."

The lesson had promised to drag on through interminable hours, but halfway through Ankhrekhu stood up, glancing at the pattern of sunlight and shadows outside his window. "I think that's enough theoretical work for the day. I suggest you spend the rest on a practical demonstration of the foreign ways we've been studying."

"The delegation from Kush?" Ameni said, his long face brightening.

The priest nodded his shaven head. "Yes. This afternoon traders from the tribes of Kush are making offerings to the pharaoh in gratitude for his protecting their trade routes through Nubia. You might wish to attend."

Eagerly Ameni followed the suggestion, not just to avoid his studies but also to get a close view of the foreigners. It wasn't as good as actually venturing into foreign countries, of course, but at least it carried a hint of that sort of thing.

When, out of breath and slightly disheveled, he reached the audience chamber, the long pillared hall was already filling with members of the court. Receiving a trade delegation was hardly a major state occasion, but visitors from the far south with their outlandish clothes and odd gifts were always intriguing.

Pharaoh's portly, heavily bejeweled vizier, stalking grandly towards his place near the dais, turned and frowned in disapproval at Ameni's appearance. Hastily the prince tried to smooth his rumpled kilt. It had dried in hopeless wrinkles. In order to be less conspicuous, he slipped behind a group of harem women, whose main concern seemed to be with their own clothes and with what the visitors would wear.

When several more courtiers had crowded into the room, the court chamberlain raised his staff and announced the arrival of the pharaoh, the Living Horus, the Great God, King of Upper and Lower Egypt, Khakheperre, Son of the Sun, Senusert, Living Forever; and that of his Great Queen, Nofret.

Ameni's parents entered the hastily hushed audience chamber. The king had chosen not to wear the heavy double crown of Upper and Lower Egypt and instead wore the striped-linen headcloth and golden cobra. The queen was wearing the light filagree jewelry Ameni knew she preferred over her heavy gold and enamel necklaces. He imagined his father was grateful for the informality of the occasion. With the annoying cough he'd picked up, it would be hard to maintain the cold godlike rigidity required for state ceremonies.

Prince Senusert had been made to change into a fresh well-pleated kilt and was standing self-consciously at the edge of the dais that held his parents' thrones. Most of the other royal children clumped excitedly below him and to the side.

Rising murmurs were stilled by the herald's call and the opening of the great gilded doors. The first of the Kushites bowed deeply, then proceeded proudly up the long walkway toward the thrones.

Ameni pushed his way forward for a better look. The men were large and dark. Their hair, bound with beads and feathers, was a curly black. Their robes were bright and fringed; and several, Ameni noticed, had cheeks marked with ritual scars to show their tribes.

The first two carried large bunches of white ostrich feathers, which bounced and swayed as they walked. Another pair carried a litter weighed down with the skins of exotic animals. Then came the bearers of ebony caskets, several containing ingots of gold, the others holding rare unguents and semiprecious jewels. The women near Ameni exclaimed at these and crowded forward for a better look.

Four porters followed, struggling under a pair of enormous curved elephant tusks that brought gasps of admiration. These dissolved into chuckles at the sight of the short, squat man who followed and the even shorter little man who rode on his shoulder.

Ameni slid into the front ranks. He had heard about these little creatures. They weren't really men but animals from the mysterious woodlands south of Kush. The creature was covered with red-brown fur, except for his face, which was as wizened and wise-looking as an old man's. And his long tail curled and twisted behind him like a snake.

The little man with his monkey passenger took his place below the thrones, then turned to watch the entry of the final member of the company. This man was taller than the others, and his skin was a shiny black. But more impressive yet was the creature pacing before him at the end of a tassled leash.

Ameni had seen leopard skins before, mostly on priests, but he'd only imagined the living animal. Never had he thought it would stalk along with the power, arrogance, and beauty of a god. Its magificent spotted coat rippled and shone as if inlaid with gold and ebony. As it passed, the watching courtiers drew back with muffled exclamations of admiration and fear.

The creature's reception from the monkey, however, was altogether different. It began chattering, squealing, and jumping about on its keeper's shoulder.

The leopard did not deign to notice this until he and his keeper had joined the others before the king. Then he wrinkled his lips and snarled at the monkey, revealing great white fangs, sharp as knives.

At this the monkey broke into a frenzy of squeals. Suddenly it leaped through the air, pulling the rope from its startled keeper, and landed directly on the head of the leopard. Before the cat could react, the monkey was off again, bounding for refuge among the cluster of royal children. Snarling in rage the leopard crouched, then with rippling muscles, sprang after his assailant.

In those few seconds, Ameni seemed to see everything in slow, precise detail. Chattering in alarm, the monkey landed in the arms of Neferhent, where it struggled to hide itself. Prince Senusert jumped down from the dais and tried to untangle the little hands from her hair. Neither noticed the leopard launch himself towards them.

Without thinking, Ameni broke free of the screaming women and ran forward. Maybe he could catch the trailing leash or at least put himself between the beast and his unsuspecting cousin and brother.

The snarling blur of gold and black was nearly upon him. Then suddenly arms grappled him about the chest, and he crashed to the tile floor. Dazed, he rolled over and struggled to sit up. Children and courtiers were screaming and running, but somehow the large Kushite had grabbed the halter again. Nobody seemed to be hurt.

Angrily Ameni turned to his own assailant and was startled to see Ankhrekhu beside him on the floor, trying to straighten his priestly robes and pull his gold necklace around to the front.

"Why did you stop me?" Ameni demanded, too angry to be respectful. "He could have torn them apart."

"Possibly, but there were others to stop him. And he most certainly *would* have torn you apart if you'd taken one step closer."

"Well, it's my life!"

"No, your highness, it is not. Your life is Egypt's."

"Bah!" Ameni stood up, then helped his tutor to his feet. "I'm not the heir, the future god. What I give my life for is my choice."

"Royal princes don't always have a choice, your highness. Where duty leads, you must, in the end, follow."

Having determined that no harm had come to anyone, the

courtiers resumed their places, the royal couple returned to their thrones, and the Kushites prostrated themselves, begging forgiveness. Ameni realized, to his pleasure, that he could understand their abject speeches before they were even translated. Yet his mind kept straying back to the leopard incident.

In saving him from certain danger, his tutor had exposed his brother and cousin to possible danger. Ameni supposed that Ankhrekhu had simply been exercising his personal duty. But somehow he couldn't dismiss the uneasy feeling it gave him, as if the nets of duty were closing about him as well.

The feeling was still with him that evening when he and Senusert had crawled under the sheets on their narrow rope-strung beds and lay looking up at the deep black sky and its glittering stars. On hot nights, the two boys chose to sleep on the roof, a privilege not granted the younger denizens of the nursery.

Senusert's mind seemed to be somewhere else as well. "Kakure," he said thoughtfully.

"Huh?"

"What do you think of 'Kakure' as a throne name? 'Souls Dawning.' You always used to like that. Do you still think it sounds right?"

"Oh sure. If I had to be king, I'd still choose that. Kakure Amenemhat. But barring any more leopards rampaging your way, I won't have to worry about that sort of thing."

"No, but I will, and sooner than I thought."

Ameni felt suddenly cold.

Sensing his alarm, Senusert said. "No, no, it's not that. Father's just fine. But tonight he said he wants me to become coregent at this year's festival. He said I'm fourteen now and he became coregent with his father at about that age. But I don't know, Ameni. I'm not sure I'm ready."

"Of course you are. You wouldn't have all the duties of a full king, but you could start work on some of those things you're always planning."

"True," his brother said dreamily. Then he flipped over onto his stomach and looked at Ameni lying in the next bed. "And I've figured out the first thing I'll do. I've talked it over with Inpy the architect and with General Renseneb, and they think it might work. I'll build a canal right through the rock at the first cataract. Then nothing can stop our ships from going upriver into Nubia. We can launch a much bigger campaign against the Nubians, strengthen our forts, and have a stronger hold on the gold mines and trade routes.

"Then after we subdue the Nubians, I think I'll march into Syria like Sinuhe in the story, only for real."

"Sounds good," Ameni said sleepily. "I'd like to see Syria."

"Of course you must come with me, too. I couldn't handle all that without your help. Besides, you can speak all those outlandish languages."

His brother yawned and smiled at the picture of the two of them adventuring off into Nubia and Syria. Senusert talked on and on, his words gradually stretching out and slurring into sleep.

Ameni too was sinking warmly away when a sudden cold thought shocked him awake. If Senusert became coregent then he, Amenemhat, would become the crown prince, at least until Senusert married and produced sons of his own. And if he were crown prince, any hopes he had for real freedom and adventure would vanish like water poured on sand.

The net was closing tighter and tighter around him.

Well, he wouldn't let it! All that duty Ankhrekhu droned on about did not have hold of him yet. And he had a plan, a fantasy he always played with when duties got too boring or he had trouble falling asleep. If he was ever to turn it from daydream to reality, he realized suddenly, now might be his last chance.

He would have his adventure. And by Osiris and all the gods, no web of duty would keep him from it!

TWO

Lorna Padgett shielded her eyes against the glare of the sun and its metal-bright reflection on the surface of the Nile. She would not wear dark glasses; only tourists did that. For her, the baking heat and blinding glare meant one thing: She was home.

As long as she could remember, Egypt had been her home. Most of her education had come in afternoon sessions in their Cairo apartment, or in tents on one of her father's excavations. She'd pursued these lessons with great diligence so as to ward off more formal education.

Even so, her widowed father would occasionally emerge

from his world of archaeology long enough to feel a wave of guilt about somehow neglecting his daughter. Then she'd be sent for a stint at an English-speaking school in Cairo or, worse, to that boarding school in England.

Those English stays were grim exile. What did she care about "interacting with one's peers" or "acquiring social graces"? She already knew most of the academic subjects as well as her classmates, and the latest soap opera or rock stars were about as boring and irrelevant to her as Cromwell's squabbles with Parliament. More so really, because of the way her peers drooled over them. Anything they liked was automatically suspect. Not fair perhaps, but she didn't want to be fair. She wanted to be herself.

She had grown up speaking Arabic as soon as English and reading Egyptian hieroglyphics as early as her ABCs. And she'd learned the ancient Egyptian king lists way before she'd mastered all the Henrys, Richards, and Georges of English history. When her schoolmates dreamed of becoming models or video stars, she dreamed of discovering a treasure like Tutankhamon's or of translating a hieroglyphic inscription that would shed gleaming new light on some murky part of Egypt's past.

She looked up from the hypnotic ripple of sunlight on water, to where the east bank of the river slowly passed by their boat. Her scowling thoughts of English school faded like a bad dream. Here was the stuff that made her daydreams. The bleaching sun of midday had beaten all depth and color from the scene, until the cliffs, clustered villages, and even the narrow green strip of crops and palm trees looked like some faded painting on an ancient crumbling wall. Out here on the river, the steady northern breeze kept the heat bearable, drying the sweat as soon as it formed on her bare freckled arms. In the old days, it would have billowed the bright striped sails above a graceful wooden boat. It took great effort of imagination to insert that image in place of the drab, rusty tug now shrugging and coughing its way upstream. Still, whatever the century, this was Egypt. She hugged herself happily.

The other passengers were mostly local people using the old boat as a convenient bus between villages. The few tourists aboard had been grumbling for hours about having chosen the cheaper milk run instead of the glamorous cruise ship that stopped only at major attractions. She looked at the gabbling group with studied scorn. But she was too happy at the moment even for good scorn. She should pity these people, really. They weren't lucky enough to be Egyptians.

The boat was drawing closer to the east bank now, and Lorna could see a group of children playing by the crumbling quay in front of their village. One girl, maybe her own age, stood up and waved at the boat before returning to her game.

Lorna sighed. Self-illusion shattered again. She might feel at home here, but she hardly looked it. Not the way that girl did with her skin the color of sun-baked earth and hair a long glossy black. The only color in her own pale skin came from freckles which the sun had spread over it like old coffee stains. And her short, frizzy hair was the color of the rust patches on the boat's hull. Her eyes, instead of dark, mysterious pools, were the same muddy blue-green as the water churning by them. She sighed again. No one could really mistake her for an exotic daughter of the Nile.

Their boat was pulling into port, a village not much larger than the others they had passed, but with a slightly more substantial quay. The pale sandstone cliffs that for endless miles had paralleled the river dropped away here. Behind this village stretched a great wadi, a dry river course that cut like a jagged scar through the eastern mountains, forming an ancient route to the Red Sea.

Lorna left the railing and went to fetch her bag. It was heavy, filled mostly with books. Her father would have the clothes and other gear she needed at their camp. She was glad her wretched school had good long winter breaks so she wouldn't miss all of this year's digging season. With any luck, her father might be so wrapped up in the excavation he'd forget to send her back for the spring term.

The boat bumped into the wharf, ropes were thrown and made fast while orders and greetings were yelled back and forth. The tourists huddled protectively together, taking pictures of the quaint mud-brick village. Several of the local passengers crowded toward the gangplank and worked their way down, waving and calling in Arabic to people on the bank. With a deliberately pitying look at the foreigners, Lorna joined the jostling natives.

At the bottom of the ramp, several small children crowded around her, asking pathetically for money. When she answered them in fluent, negative Arabic, they giggled and moved in search of a more gullible target. She smiled. They knew a native when they heard one. From the village café further up the bank, floated the whining music of a transistor radio. Several of her fellow passengers headed that way, talking about glasses of tea. She flinched as a scruffy yellow dog barked at her then, duty done, trotted off to bark at someone else.

"Lorna, over here!"

Looking up, she saw a slight, ruddy-faced man with fading red hair and the usual shapeless cloth cap clamped over his bald spot.

"Daddy!" She hoisted up her bag and eagerly started through the thinning crowd toward him. "You came to meet me yourself."

"Had to send off a telegram, so why not? And we've been making such wonderful finds, Lorna! An absolutely marvelous site!"

He grabbed her bag with one hand, gesticulating with the other as they walked along. "Had no idea when we started here it would turn out so well. It's a whole village buried partly under an avalanche. A quarry workers' village, mostly Eleventh and Twelfth Dynasty. There was a lot of quarrying done up the wadi here."

That was typical of her father, Lorna thought as she trotted beside him towards the Landrover. Immediately launching into his enthusiasms. No "How was the trip?" or "How's England doing?" Just the dig and the new discoveries. But she wouldn't have him any other way. She was home again.

Soon they were jolting up the broad wadi, following not so much a road as a series of faint tire-tracks running in the same direction over the hard gravelly earth. Dr. Padgett talked on enthusiastically, while Lorna half listened and half studied the desolate landscape. The dry air shimmered in the heat, sometimes casting phantom pools of water along their route. This was her first excavation away from the Nile Valley, and the farther east they moved, she decided, the more lunar everything looked.

The wind-sculpted ridges, folding down toward them on both sides, seemed bare of all life. But occasionally there were patches of coarse grass or clusters of spindly acacia trees that marked a well or small village. Once they glimpsed a pair of fleeing gazelles, and later in a side wadi saw the beehive domes of several bedouin tents. Camels and a small herd of rangy cattle wandered nearby, tended by several dusty children who grinned and waved as the Landrover rumbled past.

Not far beyond this migrant settlement, they turned into another side wadi. Lorna craned to look out the front window and watch the towering cliffs close in on both sides. The west face loomed in purple shadow, but the eastern cliffs still glowed a warm red in the afternoon sun.

"Well, here we are!" her father said proudly when the engine finally sputtered into silence. At the base of the eastern cliff, the low sun highlighted the waffle pattern of an excavation grid. The diggers who would be swarming purposefully over the site in the cool of the morning had returned to the cluster of bedouin tents she could see further up the wadi. From there, the hot dry breeze brought voices calling in Arabic and the growling gurgle of a protesting camel.

From the canvas tents near the foot of the cliffs, a number of staff, English and Egyptian, hurried out to greet them, most of them known to Lorna from past seasons. Again she felt the warm flush of homecoming.

After a spate of greetings, her father showed her their tent. "Our old green one finally gave out—canvas completely rotted. The small finds are being done in that red tent over there. There're quite a lot of them. That landslide apparently covered the place sometime during the middle of the Twelfth Dynasty, and the quarrying operation was abandoned right afterward. Some of the quarries seem to have been abandoned even earlier. Most of the good stone was gone by then anyway.

"We're finding lots of everyday things—beads, pots, work

tools. I hope you want to do small finds again. We've a good pot restorer this year, but nobody as good as you at registering small finds. No inscriptions for you yet, though we live in hope."

The more her father talked, the happier Lorna felt. This was a good site all right, but better yet, her father was so excited about it, he really might forget she was supposed to leave again in a little over a month. We live in hope, indeed.

As the days went on, Lorna felt as happy as a lizard basking in the sun. The only marring shadow was the creeping calendar date when she was to return to the cold and damp of a British winter, the oppression of boring lessons, and the company of people who made her feel both awkwardly inadequate and loftily superior.

Angrily, she shoved the shadow to the back of her mind, and to keep it there threw herself fully into the excavation work. From dawn to midday, men wielded picks and shovels, and boys carried baskets of dirt away from the cuttings. When the remains of a house were reached, work slowed to the careful use of trowels and whisk brooms. Occasionally Lorna helped with this or with sifting the dirt for small items like beads and potsherds. Her main task, however, was in the tent, cataloging and drawing small finds. When her father was around, she'd haul out the books she'd brought and ostentatiously study them between spells of work. Surely he would see how little she needed formal schooling.

Her world settled into a self-contained routine. The only inpingement from the outside came every few days when jets of the Egyptian Air Force streaked overhead. Obviously they were trying out either new planes or new pilots, and occasionally a show-off would swoop low over the wadi to impress the dust grovelers and scatter their camels and goats. The workmen always reacted with shouts of mixed anger and admiration.

Usually, however, afternoons were quiet and devoted to work in the tents. On one such, Lorna made an elaborate show of turning from drawing beads to reading a textbook on medieval France. But soon she pushed it gloomily aside. Her father, engrossed in a book of his own, hadn't noticed a thing. And anyway she didn't care about medieval France any more than she did about the dull chattering students she'd be studying it with in a few weeks. The only interesting part in this French stuff was the chapter on monasteries and nunneries. In those days, young people could shut themselves away from the world, devoting themselves to what they considered important, and they weren't made fun of or dissuaded but praised and admired. She sighed. Wrong century again, Lorna.

"Daddy," she said suddenly. Her father, deep into an old excavation report, only grunted.

"Daddy, you don't have to send me back to England next week. This is such an important site, I really should stay here. I brought all my schoolbooks with me. I can keep up."

"Mmm." He looked up and blinked as if just stepping from a cave. "No, Lorna, I think you should go back. A girl your age really shouldn't lead such a lonely life. Of course, you're a wonderful help to me, you always are. But it's selfish of me to keep you here, away from your contemporaries."

"But I'm not lonely! And those 'contemporaries' and I have absolutely nothing in common. We don't even have anything to talk about. It's *there* that I'm lonely, not here."

Dr. Padgett smiled weakly. "I know, Lorna. I've made this sort of thing my life, and it's fine for me. But a pretty girl like you really ought to have more options. Let's just give that school a little more of a chance."

He returned to his book. Lorna could have squealed with frustration, but knew better than to argue anymore now. She scowled at her own book for another minute, then quietly stood up and slipped out of the tent.

The breeze that fretted at her hair was hot and dry. But already the worst heat of the day was lifting. She'd go exploring. Real things like rocks and heat and scuttling lizards would at least keep her mind on the present, not the cold, wet future.

She'd already explored most of the area around their camp and the ancient village. But she had never really gone up to the quarries that tunneled into the hillside. She'd found those dark eyelike openings in the cliffs rather brooding and hostile. But she felt rather brooding and hostile herself at the moment, so they seemed the perfect goal.

Her father and others had been to the lower ones. They'd found a few broken work tools and even some graffiti scratched into the rock. Maybe she could find something exciting like that.

She skirted the now quiet excavation and found the faint path scribbling up the cliff towards the caves that were the quarry openings. The silence around her seemed vast. It was still too hot for hawks to be circling and calling in the high blue sky. The only sound came from the furnace-dry wind rasping over rock and gravel. This kind of loneliness she loved.

Outside the first cave, she saw a group of hieroglyphics scratched into the rocks. Someone had highlighted the figures with chalk for better photography. For a moment she studied the simple inscription. "Inyotef made this"—the ancient equivalent of "Kilroy was here." Hesitantly she reached out and touched the carvings. Four thousand years ago, Inyotef, a stoneworker, had written this so he might be remembered. She felt the same tingling awe that always came when she touched the past in this way.

Almost reluctantly she left the inscription, with its plea for immortality, and stepped into the cool darkness of the quarry mouth. She let her eyes slowly adjust to the gloom, wanting to put off using the artificial glare of her flashlight as long as possible.

Gradually she could make out the tunneled galleries and the massive pillars of natural stone left to hold up the roof. As mines went, this seemed to be a relatively shallow one, and soon she returned to the sun and moved farther up the cliff to what had obviously been a much more important quarry. Not far in, however, it was blocked by fallen rock, and after a brief exploration she returned to the entrance. Leaning against a smooth, cold rock, she considered whether to go back to camp.

Sunlight gleamed off the iridescent back of a beetle. Scuttling through the dust, it looked like an ancient jeweled scarab. She told it so in ancient Egyptian. She loved using that long-dead language. It was her own special, secret language. She used it to tell off her schoolmates, and the more they treated her oddly for it, the more she used it on them. Now she commented again on the little bug's beauty as it hurried along a faint trail between the rocks.

And there was a trail. She could see it now. Long disused and rock-strewn, it traced its way farther up the cliff. She stood up and followed it, climbing higher and higher as the mountain folded back on itself. Finally the faint track led to a third dark gash in the cliff.

Stepping gratefully into the cool opening, she could tell that this man-made cave was larger and higher than the others. It also lacked the dry, sterile smell of stone. The air reeked with an odor like burning rubber. She wondered what it was. A few steps into the gloom, and the stone began to feel soft and slippery under her feet. She switched on her flashlight, playing it over the oozy floor, then apprehensively up to the ceiling.

The ceiling moved. It rustled and shivered as if muscles were twitching under some dark animal hide. Suddenly bits broke away and began darting through the air, squeaking and chittering. Bats!

She hated bats! Her schoolmates kidded her about liking to hang around with mummies. She didn't mind mummies; they were dead. But bats weren't.

With a squeal of her own, she threw an arm over her head, ducked low, and ran. Her flight took her further into the darkness. She stumbled over a stone floor no longer slippery with droppings and finally collided with a pillar.

The feel of the cool, rough stone calmed her down. She liked animals, all animals except large growling dogs—and bats. At least there weren't any this far into the quarry. They clustered near the entrance so they could pour out at evening in a squeaking, flittering cloud.

She flashed her light over the pillar, its irregular surface faceted by tools of bronze some four thousand years earlier. Courage restored, she began exploring further back.

At first a dim gray haze filtered in from the entrance, but when she turned a sharp corner, that was gone. She had only her flashlight. The galleries of this mine had been cut deep into the heart of the mountain. In her shifting light, the remaining rock glowed a deep blood red. Cold began seeping from the mountain's bones into hers. The silence about her was absolute, the silence of the tomb.

At the end of this gallery, a small side room jutted off. Hesitantly she stepped into it. A dead end, it seemed. She shivered. She had no fear of the dark, but this was more than dark. In this black crypt, so remote from the outside world, it was easy to feel the presence of other worlds. Perhaps one inhabited by those strange animal-headed gods worshiped by the diggers of these quarries.

She shook herself. She'd grown up with things Egyptian. Even their weird mythology was more familiar than frightening. Resolutely she turned back toward the entrance, then jumped with alarm. A thunderlike boom rang dully through the mountain.

She almost laughed in relief. Those hotshot Egyptian pilots were buzzing them again, sonic boom and all. They must have shot by much lower and faster than usual. She wondered if the pilot would be bawled out for such a stunt.

The reverberations rolled through the mountain, sinking finally into a murmur. But they were followed by other sounds. A distant rumble, a dry shifting and grinding, then a great clattering roar. The entire mountain was collapsing. An avalanche!

THREE

 Ameni woke as the last stars were fading into the pearling expanse of predawn sky. At first there was nothing but the beauty and the refreshing chill of an early breeze. From some distant temple, chanting rose like incense as priests prepared to greet the returning sun god. A peaceful, perfect morning. Then he remembered.

The threatening claws of duty tightened around him again. But now he could hold them off. He had a plan.

Sitting up quietly, he looked over at his brother, still asleep in the bed beside him. They shared the same features, all right, and some of their father's as well. Chins were strong, and cheekbones high as a cat's. But Ameni was afraid their ears resembled more the elephants of the south. He rather wished that they stuck a little closer to the head. Everything else was all right, except perhaps for the mouth. Even in sleep, it turned down at the edges as if in a perpetual frown. But maybe that was part of what made their father such a daunting and effective ruler. Everyone coming before him was sure he disapproved of them.

Senusert snuffled in his sleep and rolled over. Ameni sighed. He felt a little guilty. He and his twin had always shared everything; but he didn't think he should tell about his plan. Though the older prince had accepted the fact that he would be king someday and was planning his life around it, he couldn't be immune from some desire to escape his duties. Yet as crown prince, he could not do anything rash. So his twin would just have to have adventure for both of them.

For the next days, palace routine went as usual. The king's cold turned his perpetual semblance of ill humor into the real thing, so courtiers and advisors approached him carefully. The nursery, though, was only slightly subdued, and the two princes went about their regular studies.

Ameni, however, had a hard time keeping his mind on the language of the Hittites or the customs of the Sea People. His thoughts were filled with his plan.

Gradually he collected the things he needed and hid them in a chest under his downstairs bed. There was a plain kilt and headcloth of coarse woven linen, reed sandles unadorned with gold or jewels, a bow and quiver of arrows, also with no adornment, a favorite throwing stick, a water skin, and a bag of dried dates. From his jewel box, he took several gold rings and a small bronze dagger and wrapped them in a scrap of linen.

In the sleepy heat of one afternoon when even the flies seemed to be dozing, Ameni strolled out into the palace grounds to examine the various walls. The cubbyhole, his favorite hiding place as a small child, was still there. When their father had built a new garden next to an earlier one, a small cul-de-sac had been formed. With much straining and some scraped elbows, he managed to work his way up the narrow shaft formed by the joining walls. From the top, he peered into the royal granary. Perfect.

In the evenings now before crawling into his open-air bed, Ameni sat on the rooftop studying the movements of the guards below. In unvarying routine, they paced the outer walls that enclosed the royal compound—garden, granary, and all.

Finally there came a day when he felt ready. Excitement glowed in him until he was sure everyone could see it. Yet, incredibly, no one seemed to. Right after supper, he slipped into his room, removed his little hoard from the chest, filled the water skin, and with much skulking and hiding from servants, snuck up to the roof and slid everything under his bed there.

It seemed to take forever for his brother to fall asleep that night. He talked on and on about his plans for Nubia, and several times Ameni was tempted to tell him about his own more modest plans. But he kept still, and finally Senusert drifted off to sleep.

Ameni lay quiet a while longer, his heartbeat almost drowning the sound of his brother's steady breathing. Then silently he slipped out of bed. Pulling out his hidden things, he donned the plain clothing, slung the quiver, bow, water skin, and bag of dates over his shoulders, then stuffed the small packet with rings and dagger under the tight waistband of his kilt. The throwing stick he stuck there as well, although it jabbed awkwardly when he bent over.

Finally he took up the scrap of papyrus he had prepared in secret with a carefully inked message. "Brother Senusert," he had written, "no one should worry on my account. I am leaving for a while but will be careful and come to no harm. When I return, I will have exciting adventure tales to tell, like Sinuhe after adventuring in the wild lands of the north. Amenemhat."

He wedged this note into the inlaid woodwork at the foot of his brother's bed, then crept to the edge of the roof. The roofs of the palace fell away from here like a random series of steps. Silent as a cat, he dropped from one to another, remembering the time he had done it when he was much younger; that adventure had sent his nurses into screaming horror.

He landed with a light thump on the trodden dirt of a garden path, and like a shadow he sped along it. In the soft darkness overhead, a myriad stars winked like silent conspirators and gave him a faint, silvery light. Panting more from excitement than exertion, he reached the concealing niche where the garden walls joined. Slowly he began levering himself up, feet against one wall, back against the other. He peered cautiously over the top. The guard on the far outer wall was maybe ten seconds from the next tower. When his pacing took him through it, there'd be a moment when he could see nothing on the granary side.

The figure vanished behind the stonework. Ameni was down and running like a rat behind the beehive domes of the storage bins. He reached the back gate, scrambled up its latticework inner side and flung himself over. The palace defenses were made to keep people out, not in.

Now he was free. Trying not to act like a fugitive, he walked along the narrow deserted street into the main part of town.

Itowe was comparatively new. Most of it had been built since his great-great-grandfather, Amenemhat I, had moved the capital from southern Thebes to this spot midway between the joined lands of Upper and Lower Egypt.

Still, in those few years, the city had sprawled into a great warren of streets, with brick homes ranging from great white villas to miserable hovels. Ameni had never been outside the palace except for processions, temple visits, or official royal excursions like building inspections or hunts. He knew he was bound to get lost. But that was part of the adventure.

On one winding street, he stopped in alarm as a man suddenly lurched out of a doorway in front of him. But clearly this was no robber, only a very unsteady drunk. The man wove his way down the street bawling out over and over again a bawdy song about a man returning to his house and finding a stranger in his bedroom. It was hardly the sort of song princes hear from palace musicians, and for that reason Ameni loved it. He followed the man until he had learned it, then sang the catchy little thing under his breath until he was way out of town on the southwestern road.

He planned to walk until dawn and then hide somewhere and get some sleep. People wouldn't realize he was gone until Senusert showed them the note, as he was bound to do once they started worrying. Then they'd probably start looking for him down by the river or on roads leading north. He'd purposefully laid that clue about Sinuhe and adventures in Syria so they'd do that. He figured if he actually headed north towards the Delta and the sea, he would surely be caught. Instead he'd hide out in the Fayum, make a living for himself somehow, then later head north to Syria or perhaps south to Kush.

Pleased and excited and singing the bawdy drunkard's song, the prince walked briskly along the road until the eastern horizon began graying then streaking itself with gold. The sight was beautiful, but sleepiness fogged his vision, and his feet were becoming heavier at every step. Gratefully he spied a low square building not far west of the road.

From the modest pylons and carvings in front, he decided it was a mortuary temple, probably for some local noble who was actually buried in a tomb among the western cliffs. But the place looked old and poorly maintained. He was sure the soul of the departed would not begrudge a tired prince a little rest. He crept inside, curled up behind a stone offering-table, and was soon asleep.

When he awoke, the angle of sunlight slicing across the dark entryway showed it was late morning. Ameni was achingly hungry. He dipped into the bag at his side and pulled out a handful of dried dates. Sucking on one until it softened, he thought about what he should do next.

Surely these dates wouldn't last him very long. He would have to find some village where he could exchange a ring or work for food, then head off into the Fayum. He spit out the date stone, popped another date into his mouth and stood up. Sun was leaking into the little temple through several holes in the roof. Clearly the dust-strewn altar had seen no offerings for the welfare of the departed soul in a long time.

It was a shame that this poor man's immortality should be endangered by neglect from those he had endowed to maintain his temple and make perpetual offerings. The lands given to support this task were surely rich enough, but the trustees were probably spending all the profits on themselves.

Ameni reached again into his bag and placed three dates on the altar. He wondered how long a soul could live on the spirit value of three dates. He sighed, and slipped out into the sunlight.

In the prosperous-looking fields around him, several men and women were working. He ducked out of sight behind a wall, but not before one fat man spied him and began yelling and lumbering his way.

"Halt, you young scoundrel! How dare you enter the mortuary temple of Lord Ptahotep?"

Pricked with anger, Ameni slowed his flight and turned to face the man. He could see from the robes that this was a mortuary priest. "I needed rest. And if your good Lord Ptahotep gave me shelter, then I gave him a funerary offering in exchange—which is a good deal more than you've done for your lord of late."

"Why, you impudent brat! I'll teach you to preach to your betters!" The fat man brought up his walking stick and lowered it with a stinging smack on Ameni's shoulders.

The prince stood dumbfounded, not so much from the pain as from the fact that someone had struck him, something that had never happened in his life. The pain of a second blow snapped him into action. He reached up, grabbed the stick, wrenched it from the man's hand and delivered a swat to the fellow's shaven head.

The priest bellowed like an ox, and those field hands not already moving started running their way. Ameni looked around, threw down the stick, and began running over the fields, his amulet whacking rhythmically against his chest. The farm workers changed course and took up the chase. Hound and hares. And he was the hare—for real.

His pursuers outnumbered him, but clearly they had little enthusiasm for a race in the midday heat, no matter what indignities had been heaped on their fat priest. When Ameni finally reached the shelter of an acacia thicket, they gave up and went back to their work, glad for the morning's diversion.

Seeing he was no longer pursued, Ameni slowed to a walk. Now that it was over, the incident seemed almost an adventure. Well, take adventure as it comes, he told himself with an attempt at jauntiness.

Still, that stick had hurt. He rubbed his bare shoulders to find two raised welts already snaking across his skin. He would need to stay clear of villages for a while in case word got out that there was a priest-beater on the loose.

He avoided roads now and rationed his dates, but the water he drank up before the afternoon was half through. Finally he stopped and asked an old woman if he could refill his water skin. She was squatting outside her brick farmhouse methodically weaving reeds into mats. Standing up, she examined him disapprovingly, but finally pointed to a large clay pot kept cool in the shade of a spindly tree. Ameni refilled his water skin, then thanking the surly woman, continued on, stopping occasionally to pull out long acacia thorns that had slipped past his sandles and jabbed into his feet. The glow of adventure was beginning to wear off, but he was sure things would be better tomorrow.

As he trudged on, he took his thoughts off his own discomfort by watching hawks circle over the fields he passed. Now there was real freedom. It would be nice if the Great God

Pharaoh, the Living Horus, had the power to change himself into Horus's living symbol, the hawk. Then it might almost be worthwhile becoming king. He wondered what sort of power or new senses a man actually got when he became the Living Horus. He'd be a god, after all.

When one king died and became the incarnation of Osiris in the otherworld, his eldest son became the incarnation of Horus, son of Osiris, and ruled as Egypt's living god until he too died and became one with Osiris and all those earlier kings. But it really couldn't be so wonderful, being the Living Horus, or his father, great king as he was, wouldn't always seem so careworn. No, godhood was not to be envied, if all it meant was being tied to heavier duties.

That evening, Ameni avoided villages and mortuary temples though his date bag was nearly empty and his stomach howled with hunger. He was about to make himself a sleeping place in a dry irrigation ditch, when he caught a flickering glimpse of a campfire in a dark grove of palms. He crept closer and picked up the tantalizing smell of roast duck. As if pulled by magic incantations, he found himself drawn closer and closer to the fire.

Without seeming to look up, the thinner of two ragged men called into the darkness. "There's enough duck, bread, and wine for a third traveler, should one chance this way."

Gratefully, Ameni stepped out into the fireglow. "I can add a few dates to the feast, but nothing more."

"Keep your dates, boy, we have food aplenty," said the stouter of the two. "Sit and join us."

Ameni did and soon was chewing succulent roast duck and wiping grease from his chin with a generous hunk of bread.

His companions introduced themselves as two adventurers wandering wherever work could be had, up and down the

Two Lands and into lands beyond. Ameni's eyes glowed at the wonders they told of, some no doubt pure fantasy but exciting nonetheless. Finally sleep overtook him, and he curled up like a contented cat by the fire.

He woke to the odd sensation of something moving about his waist. He slipped a hand down and met another hand. A gruff voice laughed above him.

"Thought you seemed a little too bright and quick to be some runaway apprentice. Part of a tomb robbers' gang, that's what we had you pegged for. Not far wrong, were we?" The red glow of embers glinted off the fine bronze dagger and the two gold rings the thin man held in his hand.

The second man on the edge of the fire circle chuckled, and Ameni saw that he held his bow and arrows.

"Give those things back to me, both of you! I need them."

"Now, don't we sound regal, though? Well, we need them, too. The weapons are nicely made and should bring something. But these rings now. . . . Care to tell us where you happened to find them? A nice untampered-with tomb, maybe? Some rich man's carelessly unlocked house?"

Ameni lowered his hand to the ground and the wooden throwing stick he'd used as a pillow. In an instant, he grabbed it and flung it at the thin man. It glanced off his forehead, sending him staggering back with a yelp.

"Why you little monster!" the man yelled and lunged forward. Ameni scrambled to his feet and ducked back into the darkness.

"Leave off," the second man said, as the first started in pursuit. "He'll run circles around you in these trees at night." He laughed and pulled his friend away. "Besides, someday the uppity brat might become king of the local tomb robbers, and we'd want him to remember us for having dined him so royally."

Angrily Ameni started to follow as they headed off through the trees. But he hadn't gone far when he realized it was hopeless. They were two strong, grown men, and they had left him weaponless. He fumbled over the ground among the crackling palm fronds until he found his throwing stick. But even this wouldn't be much good against the two of them. He'd just have to continue on towards the Fayum and hope to exchange his labor for food. His gold was gone.

Sullenly he trudged through the following day, finally stopping in the middle of the afternoon at a good-sized village. He wandered down the main street smelling food on every side and feeling increasingly starved. It was local market day, but though he looked into each of the stalls in the craftsmen's section, none seemed to house a craft of which he had any useful knowledge. The bronzesmith was hammering and heating his metal in ways that looked as mysterious as any temple ritual. Ameni's only knowledge of clay-working came from forming crude lumpy animals in the nursery, so pot-making was out. And basket-weaving looked even more complicated. Then he saw the answer: a scribe.

The old man was seated cross-legged under an awning in front of his home. A customer squatted before him, slowly dictating the words he wanted in his letter. Using his tautly stretched kilt as a table, the scribe deftly wrote them down, occasionally dipping his pen into the ink pallet at his side.

Ameni moved up and looked over the scribe's shoulder. The papyrus that the customer had provided was of poor quality, and the pen quavered unevenly over the surface as it recorded the hieroglyphs. But the man's hand was good, Ameni could tell.

When the letter was finished, the customer rolled it up proudly and presented the scribe with a leaf-wrapped honeycomb, dripping sweetness. Ameni's mouth watered painfully.

Alone again, the scribe looked up at him. "Are you wanting something written, young man?"

"Me? Oh no. But I could write for you, if you'd like. I mean, if you need an assistant or someone just to spell you while you go inside and have your supper." He sighed. "I can smell it now."

The old man stood up and looked him over doubtfully. "You're a scribe then? Aren't you a little young to be out of training?"

"Well, I'm not exactly a scribe, but I have a very clear hand. You can see if you give me a try."

The scribe studied him a moment more, then chuckled. "All right. As you guessed, my supper is ready. I'll join my wife for it, and you can stay out here and do any job that may come my way during that time."

As Ameni thanked him, the old man picked up his dripping honeycomb and stepped inside. The boy looked longingly after the honey, then sat cross-legged on the mat and waited hopefully for customers.

For a long while none came, and Ameni was afraid the only service he'd perform to justify asking for food would be keeping the old scribe's mat warm. He wondered if he should make some offering to Thoth, the ibis-headed god of scribes whose little wooden figure sat in a small shrine beside his mat. But he didn't even have one withered date to give.

A thin old woman hobbled up finally, stopped, and looked at him skeptically. "Are you Sisatet, the scribe?"

"Uh no, not me. He's inside. But I'm his very capable substitute. Do you have something you wish written, venerable mother?"

Slightly mollified, she squatted down. "I have a prayer I need written. I want to leave it at the shrine of Sobek, the crocodile god. Can you write it?"

Ameni could see that she had brought no papyrus, but there was a pile of smoothed potsherds beside him, obviously meant for writing on.

"Certainly. What do you wish to say?"

"Well, I don't know the proper words to make a god listen. But last year my son and grandson went fishing in the swamps. They had done that every day, but this time they never returned. I fear some accident befell them, and I have mourned them for a year. But their bodies were never found—perhaps the crocodiles ate them—and we could give them no proper burial. So now not only are their bodies lost, but their souls as well. Without burial and proper offerings, what chance have they to attain the afterworld? And when I go there, as I must soon, it will be lonely without them."

Ameni was shaken by the poor woman's sadness. All he could think of to comfort her was to do what she asked. He picked up a large potsherd, dipped his pen in the water and black ink, and carefully began writing. The figures flowed quickly over the smooth surface. Finally he stopped and read the prayer back to her.

"Most powerful and merciful god, Sobek, lord of the swamps and those who dwell therein. I commend to your care the souls of two who have labored in your realm." He paused, asked the woman for their names, wrote them in, then continued. "Please intercede for your two faithful servants so that their bereft souls may attain the peace of everlastings."

Handing the woman the sherd, he asked, "Will that do?"

He was startled to see tears running down her wrinkled cheeks "Oh, yes. Surely the god will answer such an eloquent plea. Thank you, thank you." She placed three large duck eggs before him and hurried off clutching her treasured prayer.

Ameni looked hungrily at the eggs, then felt someone behind him. He turned and found the scribe.

"A fine hand indeed, and even I could hardly have written such an appropriate prayer. You mentioned something about wanting work?"

Before Ameni could answer, a woman's voice called from inside the house. "Gracious gods, Sisatet, don't talk business now. Can't you see the lad is famished? Even young scribes can't work on empty stomachs."

The man laughed and led him to a plentiful meal of beans and bread and crisp fresh leeks, with sweet honey to follow. During the meal, Ameni was too busy eating to talk much, but he did think. He wouldn't mind working with Sisatet, though being a village scribe was hardly the adventure he sought. But this place was really not far enough from the river and from possible searchers from the palace.

In the end when the offer was made, he said he could only remain one day since he had business elsewhere. He figured they too probably thought him a runaway apprentice. But they gave him a comfortable bed that night and the next, and during the day he earned his keep writing several messages for villagers and local farmers. On the following day, the couple urged him to stay. But when he insisted he must go, they sent him off with a full bag of food and a large water-flask.

That next morning's hike brought him close to the mouth of the Fayum, that great swampy area in the west, which recent kings had begun reclaiming for farm land by impounding some of the seasonal water into a lake. But as he neared the wadi that led there, Ameni held back.

On a prominent ridge, he could see the triangular shape of his father's pyramid and the pillared mortuary temple further to the east. They were nearly finished now. He was surprised how much progress had been made in the months since the last royal inspection. He dared not pass too close, he realized, because some of the workmen or engineers might recognize him. Suppose Inpy, the royal architect, were there?

No, he would have to cut through the hills instead. He turned inland and began making his way along ibex trails through the rocks. Slowly the view of the pyramid fell behind him.

It would be a grand structure when completed. Not as huge, of course, as the great pyramids further north built by the kings of the Fourth and Fifth Dynasties. But those had taken so much effort to build that the kings had practically drained the nation's wealth to insure their immortality.

And it hadn't worked anyway. Ankhrekhu had told him that every one of those old pyramids had been robbed, some even with the complicity of priests. The very thought made him uneasy. It seemed that great kings could be no more assured of immortality than poor fishermen lost in a swamp.

He slogged on through the heat of the day, glad of the food and water he had with him. He knew he should find a shady spot and rest while the sun was at its height. But the sight of his father's pyramid had disturbed him as it never had before. It was as if the shadow of royal mortality were pursuing him into the wilderness.

Finally near evening, he sank in exhaustion onto a flat ledge of rock. The harsh patterns of sun and shadow had softened with evening, and a cool reviving breeze blew from the north. Stretching below him was the broad misty green of the Fayum basin. Nearly beneath his ledge, on a shore of swampy water stood a little village, its homes made not of bricks but of bent reeds. Already cookfires were wafting columns of purple smoke into the evening sky.

Ameni leaned back and looked up into that sky. High above, a great hawk was circling, its feathers golden in the setting sun. He watched the bird as it wheeled majestically above him, spiraling dizzily in diminishing circles. Suddenly with a piercing cry the bird beat its wings and soared off westward towards the golden horizon.

Ameni stood up to watch its progress and was hit by a sudden dizziness. His head ached and his sight swirled from confusion into darkness. He slumped to the rock, overbalanced, and slid over the edge and down the rough slope.

FOUR

For a moment, Lorna stood frozen as the rock bucked and cracked around her. That wretched jet had set off an avalanche. And now she was in the middle of a collapsing mountain!

In panic she sprinted for the opening of the side gallery. Above her the rock ceiling creaked and groaned. With a shuddering crack, a huge slab of stone crashed into her path. Coughing in a cloud of dust, she stumbled backwards. The rock was shivering all around her. She'd be crushed or buried alive!

Terrified, she huddled against the far wall, her arms flung

over her head. Instantly she thought of the few skeletons found crushed in the remains of their houses, buried in that earlier avalanche. Her skeleton probably wouldn't be found for another four thousand years.

Suddenly the wall behind her quivered, buckled, and abruptly gave way. She tumbled over backwards in a shower of dust and rock. Hopeless now, she lay listening to the receding rumbles, waiting for some great rock to fall and crush out her life.

But it never came. With one hand she tentatively brushed debris from her face and opened her eyes. Her flashlight was smashed, but there was a faint gray light. Slowly she sat up, dislodging a covering of pebbles. The wall she had been leaning against had been as much dirt as rock. And somewhere above to her right, a chink of ceiling had fallen in, revealing daylight beyond.

Almost afraid to hope, she staggered to her feet. The great scattering of dirt and scree around her was still settling into dusty silence. She looked around. Much of this loose rock must have fallen in from the surface, maybe during that ancient avalanche, and then been shifted again during this one. Leaning back, she studied the single jagged patch of light. It would be hard to reach. But she would! That was her way out. She had no intention of being a huddled skelton for future archaeologists to find.

She half looked, half felt her way around the chamber. Surely one of the walls must have fissures or ledges in the rock. The opening wasn't too far up. She ought to be able to work her way there somehow.

In the diffuse light, she could see that dirt had slumped away from at least one stone wall, making a ramp up to its hard surface. She scrambled up and began examining it.

There were some cracks here, all right, but not big ones. Nothing big enough for toe- or fingerholds. One set of cracks looked fairly regular and led up to a shallow, projecting ledge. With eager hands, she brushed away dirt and stones. The ledge was very regular, almost as if it had been carved. Halfway along, it was interrupted by a raised stone disk.

She felt its shape curiously and squinted at it in the dim light. It was a carving! A sun disk flanked by two crowned cobras. How odd to find that here. It was the sort of ornament ancient Egyptians put over doors.

Doors. She brushed more at the ledge. Surely it was carved too, an ornamental door lintel. She scarcely dared breathe. Slowly her fingers traced those straight, regular cracks. Dust fell away, and the cracks deepened. It was a distinct rectangular outline, a door set in the natural stone.

Feverishly now she scrabbled at the loose stone that concealed the lower part of the door. All thoughts of escape were gone. Howard Carter, she remembered, when he'd discovered Tutankhamon's tomb, had first found only the corner of a stair.

Digging like a dog in the scattered debris, she revealed more and more of the door. Suddenly her hand stopped. Cautiously she examined what her fingers had touched. The door crack was interrupted by a blob of hard plaster. Slowly now, she pushed more of the rubble aside.

The edge of the door was closed with a plaster seal. On it was impressed an ankh, the looped cross of eternal life. It was unbroken.

She scarcely dared allow the thought. But it beat at her with wild certainty. She had found an untouched tomb!

FIVE

When Ameni next opened his eyes, he seemed to be in a basket. There had been kittens once kept in a basket. Perhaps he was one of these. Then his mind cleared, and he realized he was lying in a hut, one of those woven-reed huts he had seen from the ledge. The ledge. He'd grown dizzy-looking at that hawk and must have fallen from the ledge. Weakly he tried to sit up and was hit by an echo of dizziness.

A short, plump woman fussed up to him and eased him back down onto the mat where he had been lying. "Easy still, lad. The sun's struck you quite a blow. You're not ready to be bouncing up just yet." She held a cup of water for him, and he drank thirstily.

"Sometimes our daughter, Ata, is a bit of a dreamer and looks around when she should be working. But it's a good thing for you she did last evening, or no one might have seen you fall from those rocks or found you before the hyenas or jackals did."

Ameni saw the face of a pretty girl peering shyly around the woman's shoulder. He found his voice.

"Thank you, Ata, for your fortunate inattention, and you, madam, for taking me in."

Within minutes the little hut was crowded with family and neighbors anxious to see and wish health to the young stranger. Soon the plump woman was scolding and flapping her hands. "Now, now, not so many. The poor lad's only just come to."

Ameni was sitting up now. "Really it's all right. I'm fine now, the dizziness is gone. Maybe I have some scratches, but I've certainly rested enough."

Nakhet, Ata's father laughed and said, "Well, you certainly were as relaxed as a brained fish when we carried you here last night. But truly lad, don't push yourself. You're welcome to stay here until you feel well enough to be on your way."

"Well," Ameni said awkwardly, fiddling at his amulet with a scratched hand, "this is more or less where I was heading."

"Oh?" the man said, squatting down ready to listen. Most of the other well-wishers had been shooed out by then.

"Yes, you see I was looking for someplace like this. I thought maybe I could help someone with fishing or hunting waterfowl. I'm pretty good with the throwing stick."

"Ah. I noticed the stick you had with you. A fine one, well balanced." The man scratched his chest while Ameni waited tensely.

"If you can use it well, we can probably use you. Our eldest son has gone off to help build the pyramid of the king, may he live forever. And I don't like it when Nisu, our youngest, goes out in the boat alone." A small boy sitting beside him grinned as broadly as a frog and scratched his ear. The man continued. "Of course, there's Heket here, but you've already met her."

He gestured toward the foot of Ameni's mat where a sleek grey cat was curled up contentedly. "Heket's the best hunting cat in the village, and if she likes you, I suppose you must be all right."

The cat had indeed taken to Ameni and slept with him nearly all day. Khu, Nakhet's wife, insisted that he stay quiet and out of the sun, and Ameni, who still felt oddly hollow, did not regret the rest, nor did he mind the soup, bread, and shy conversation Ata brought him. By the next day, however, he was feeling perfectly well, and he and Nisu, with Heket the cat, set off into the Fayum swamp.

Their boat was made of bundles of reeds tied together into a shallow leaf-shaped bowl with upturned ends. It was much like the boats Ameni, his brother, and occasionally their father had used for hunting in other more accessible parts of the Fayum. The gold banding and other royal ornaments were missing, of course.

Ameni did not feel he was much of an asset that first day. He didn't have as much experience as Nisu at fishing with a spear. His thrusts always missed, setting the boat rocking while Heket complained raucously.

The next day, however, when they flushed a flock of ducks,

Ameni's throwing stick brought one down. The stick boomeranged partway back, but the duck fell amid a wet maze of reedy hummocks. In a flash Heket vanished into the reeds, returning minutes later dragging a dead duck almost twice her size.

From then on, Ameni caught a number of ducks and other waterfowl and even improved, though hardly excelled, at fishing. Every evening they brought back their catch, which Ata and Khu smoked for later transport to one of the market towns on the Nile.

Day after day the two boys and the cat went out onto the water. Ameni began to feel that, though hardly adventurous, this life could be a satisfying one. He could almost understand someone willingly spending his life this way. But when Nisu suggested that he might do just that, and that his older sister Ata would make Ameni a perfect wife, Ameni realized things could be getting out of hand.

Ata, Ameni admitted, was a sweet, friendly, and very pretty girl. She had a lovely voice, as light and clear as a bird's when she sang over her work. But his stay here could be only temporary. As soon as he guessed it safe, he still planned to head off on some foreign adventure, returning to the palace perhaps by the end of the year. And at the palace, of course, cousin Neferhent might well figure into his life. Ata would certainly make someone a fine wife, but the stiff formality of palace life would hardly suit her as well as the wildness and beauty of the Fayum.

Ameni was brooding on this subject, not for the first time, one particularly warm day when he had been with Nakhet's family for over a week. The air was still and heavy with the rich, damp smell of rotting vegetation. Insects chirped and whined among the stalks of papyrus that rattled in an occasional hot, listless breeze. Nisu had plucked a sky blue lotus and stuck it like a banner in the prow of their boat. Now he stood motionless, poised with his spear, sweat glistening on his young bronzed back as he watched for telltale ripples in the murky water.

Standing in the stern, Ameni poled slowly and steadily, trying not to stir up the mud. He rubbed sweat from his eyes, thanking the gods he was free from formal court wigs and heavy jewelry. Gently their boat bumped into a stand of reeds, and a startled duck squawked and fluttered skyward. In one smooth motion, Ameni grabbed a throwing stick and hurled it after the bird. The two collided, and silently the duck plummeted into the reeds.

Instantly Heket was after her quarry. A moment later the waiting silence was broken by a furious yowl. Ameni poled the boat around a tuft of papyrus and saw the cat standing on a fallen log hissing and bristling at something he couldn't see.

Another push of the pole, and he saw it. A large crocodile was gliding toward the log, only the eyes and bumpy surface of its back showing above the water.

"Heket!" Ameni yelled. "Come! Don't stand there hissing."

Then he saw that the spitting cat had managed to hook her collar over a branch on the log. Despite her hissing and desperate thrashing, she was sitting bait for the crocodile.

Nisu's eyes went wide with horror. "Ameni, it's enormous. The father of all crocodiles! Quick, there's some dry land over here. Jump!"

"No, Heket's caught."

"Forget the cat. Poor thing's a goner now."

"Not the best hunting cat in the village!" Ameni protested.

56

Bringing up his long pole, he whacked the crocodile across its snout, hoping to give the cat a few more seconds to break free. It worked as far as the cat was concerned. With a violent twist the little animal wriggled loose and sprang into the reeds, while the crocodile snorted and thrashed sideways. It caught sight of the little boat then, and silently changed course.

"Jump!" Nisu shouted again as he leaped with all his might onto a grassy hummock. The boat lurched backward. Ameni fought for his balance, found it and desperately poled back towards land.

The crocodile was almost there. Ameni raised the pole again to poke it in the face, aiming for the eyes. But the animal twisted, caught the wood in its vast open mouth, and wrenched it sideways. Ameni, still clinging to the other end, was yanked overboard.

Cold water closed around him. Through its murkiness, he saw the looming dark shape of the reptile. Its mouth gaped open, showing a horrid array of daggerlike teeth.

Ameni shot out an inarticulate prayer to Sobek and any other god who would listen. Frantically he flailed backward, but hardly seemed to move. The water around him convulsed. And inexplicably the creature turned its huge body aside and swam away through the watery gloom.

Amazed, Ameni bobbed to the surface and grabbed at the overturned boat. Nisu reached a trembling arm out from the reeds. Pulling the boat to shore, he helped his friend out. Ameni stood dripping among the reeds while the boy piped, "I can't believe it. The monster almost had you, then it just turned and swam away."

Suddenly a new and unexpected voice rolled to them over the reed-clustered water. "If I had not been a believer before,

I would be now. But perhaps I should not be surprised that the crocodile left you alone, my prince, since it was a vision from the god Sobek that led me to seek you here."

Ameni stared in renewed amazement. His tutor stood in the prow of another reed boat, which Nakhet was poling in wide-eyed silence.

"Ankhrekhu . . ." the shaken prince began.

"Never mind, highness. The question of your foolhardy flight and adventuring is of no importance now. I come here on far graver matters."

Ameni listened in growing fear.

"I grieve to be the one to bring you this word, Prince Amenemhat. But the Great God, the Living Horus, has flown to his horizon. The pharaoh, your father, is dead."

SIX

Now with this incredible discovery, there was no way Lorna would allow herself to stay trapped in an old quarry. She scraped a little more gravel away from the sealed door, then doggedly examined the other stone walls for some way up. Finally, by a series of cracks and fissures, she began dragging herself like a lizard towards the jagged gray gap.

The light above her seemed to have faded. It must be near sunset. Well, she certainly wasn't going to spend the night here—not with what she had to tell.

At last, bruised and scraped, she crawled through the broken cleft of rock. The air was cool and wonderfully fresh. The sun, a vibrant bronze globe, was just slipping behind the western cliffs. Briefly the rocks around her glowed red, then they too grayed into dusk.

The underground maze seemed to have led her some distance from their camp. But here the cliff twisted into a high peak and she could look back up her own wadi as well as into a smaller one on the other side of the ridge. In the twilight below, near the bright smear of tents, she could see people moving about like panicky ants when a foot has flattened their anthill. Had anyone been hurt in the avalanche? How much had been destroyed?

Propelled by these new concerns, she bounded from rock to rock like a mountain goat, working her way down the hillside. Once at the bottom, she ran up the broad gravelly wadi toward camp.

With a sigh of relief, she saw her father in the crowd, red hair bristling around his bald patch. Somehow he must have lost his precious hat.

"Daddy! Here I am! Is everybody all right!"

Dr. Padgett spun around, burst into smiles, and ran towards her. "Lorna! Thank God you're alive! Ahmed said he saw you go up toward the quarries, and they seem to be mostly caved in now. Oh, I can't believe it. You're safe!"

"Sure I am, but what happened to everybody else? It was one of those stupid sonic booms, wasn't it? Was anyone hurt? You ought to sue the Ministry of Defense, or whatever."

"Miraculously, everyone's fine. And most of the site escaped, though one end . . . well, it's under half a mountain. Short of heavy earth-moving equipment, we'll never get at it."

"Oh that's a shame. But, Daddy, it doesn't really matter so much now."

"But who knows what might have been under there!"

"Sure, but we've found something that's much better."

"True. I've found you again, and that's really all that's important."

"No! I mean, sure that's great, but I've really found something! In the old quarry, the high one, around in the back. The door must have been covered up by that ancient avalanche, and now it's exposed again. And a little hole's been knocked in the hillside—that's how I got out—so you can get to it even if the main quarry entrance is blocked now."

"A door? What are you talking about?"

"A door in the rock with a carved lintel, and sun disk and cobras over it. And it's sealed. A plaster seal stamped with an ankh. I think . . . it may be a tomb."

The archaeologist was silent, the muscles of his face slowly tightening. When he spoke, it was almost a whisper. "A sealed tomb. Good God! Where is this thing?"

"Up there." She pointed down the wadi to the darkening cliff. "I guess we'll have to wait until morning."

"Yes, blast it all. But, oh, how wonderful! A sealed door in an old quarry. How extraordinary. Of course, it may be a storeroom, no bad thing either. But a sun disk and cobras you say? And sealed with an ankh? Not usual, surely, but it does suggest a tomb. Oh, you can't imagine how much better this makes me feel—that and finding you alive. God is good, Lorna."

And so, she decided, He was.

The next morning, Lorna led Dr. Padgett and several others up the cliff. At first she could not find the opening. But recalling the view when she had first crawled out, she clambered over the hillside until she duplicated that. The opening gaped between a tumble of rocks, small and inconspicuous.

Once lowered into the small quarry chamber with Lorna, Dr. Padgett was electrified with excitement at the sight of the door. Workmen soon joined him, and he took pictures at every stage as they cleared away the rubble. Then he studied the seal, photographed it, and with great care set about prying it away. With the seal finally freed and wrapped in a handkerchief, he directed the workmen to begin opening the door.

It took all morning. Lorna was frantic with impatience, but Dr. Padgett did not want the stonework damaged. At last, however, there had been enough wedging and shoving to allow the door to shift slightly on its dust-clogged pivots. The group of men took turns rocking and pushing until, with the sound of grinding bones, the great door opened inward.

The air that rushed out was cold and dead except for a faint odor, a memory of incense, which was gone before Lorna could name it.

With the others, she peered through the opening at the fantastic scene caught in their flashlight beams. Dark, strange shapes hunched in the chamber, painted gods processed along the walls. Her father turned to her.

"This is your discovery, Lorna. I think you should be the first to enter."

Thrilled beyond words, she stepped in front of the others. Better than Howard Carter, better than Tutankhamon. This was hers. Holding her flashlight before her, she took a deep breath. Then like a diver plunging into cold water, she stepped in.

SEVEN

Solemnly Ameni, Ankhrekhu, Nakhet, Nisu, and a subdued cat poled their way back to the village of reeds. The others there, milling around their huts, knew that something momentous was happening, but as yet had not guessed what. When they learned, they stared in awe at the boy they had already come to think of as one of their own.

Ameni, himself, was too dazed to really respond to anyone. His father was dead. He had been a good man, a good king. He should not be dead. Egypt needed him. He, Ameni, needed him.

Ankhrekhu was remote and clearly anxious to be back at the palace. He took a gold and enamel bracelet from his arm and handed it to Nakhet. "We can never repay you for caring for our prince. But with you and the gods watching out for him, he was clearly in good hands. Please accept this in personal gratitude. This headstrong pupil of mine is precious to me."

Ameni could hardly find words for leave-taking. He hugged Nakhet and Khu, then gripped Nisu's thin shoulders. After a moment, he kissed Ata on the forehead. Yes, this oasis of beauty and peace was best for her.

The priest had brought donkeys for himself and the prince plus half a dozen of the king's personal Nubian guards. For a while they rode in silence, ignoring the curious stares of those they passed. Then Ameni turned to his teacher.

"My father, did he . . . Tell me what happened."

"He died a little over a week ago. It was that cough he came down with in Nubia. One day it was much worse. His body burned with fever; he could scarcely breathe. The physicians tried everything, but he died around sunset the next day. We thought you would come back when you heard the news. When you didn't, we knew you must either be dead or isolated somewhere. I prayed to Osiris for guidance, but as I said, it was Sobek who granted me a vision of how to find you."

Ameni lowered his eyes. "I'm sorry, Ankhrekhu. My going off . . . at this time . . ."

"Humph. Well, I accept your apology, and the gods know I probably deserve it most. Your mother was worried, of course, but Senusert and Neferhent seemed more envious than upset. And your father . . . he said you were an undisciplined rogue and would be suitably punished, then he added that he was proud you'd shown so much initiative and was frankly surprised you hadn't done this sooner."

Ameni's eyes filled with tears. His tutor looked at him with his sad lopsided smile. "Your father was a great man and left us far too soon. As a priest of Osiris, I attended him those last few hours. He told me he was leaving his kingdom in good hands. And I know he was right. You are both too young for these new responsibilities, but I have faith you can handle them."

In silence, they rode past the site of the late king's pyramid. The activity around it had trebled since Ameni had passed it, not much over a week ago. His father had died that day at sunset. Heavily he recalled that day. The growing anxiety, the hawk, the dizziness. How much worse it must have been for his twin. It was he who at the pharaoh's death had become the Living Horus. Ameni shuddered, hoping he'd never have to know that weight.

The villages they passed through were in public mourning. Businesses were closed, and people in the streets wailed in ritual grief. But Senusert II had been a popular king, and Ameni suspected that much of this show was sincere.

For seventy days while the body of the king was being embalmed, his people would mourn him. Then would come the great public ceremonials that they could not deny enjoying. The funerary barge would carry the royal mummy to the port upstream, where a great procession would form. To the jangle of sistrums and the ritual wailing of mourners, the mummy, the royal family, slaves bearing lavish burial goods, and countless chanting priests would wend their way to the pyramid. Then in long ceremonies the priests and the new king, the new Living Horus, would send the new Osiris off to the afterworld, assuring him life there for all eternity. The thought of it all made Ameni shiver. It might be exciting to watch, but it would be unbearable to be part of.

The palace was in such uproar when they reached it after nearly two days' journey, that few noticed the younger prince's arrival. Ameni was relieved. But as they were dismounting from their tired donkeys, Neferhent came running from a side door and threw her arms around him. She was wearing ritual mourning dress, but he could see that the tears on her cheeks were real.

"I'm glad you're back," she said simply, "very glad, though it shouldn't have happened this way. When the world is in order again, you must tell me of your adventures. Even in this short time I'm sure you must have had some."

"I did, yes. Good ones and bad ones. But first I must go to my mother . . . and my brother."

"Yes. Senusert can use you now. I don't think he's finding the transition to life as a god very easy."

In the women's quarters, Queen Nofret greeted her son with a wordless embrace. They stayed together for a while, sharing their grief. Then Ameni left her to her attendants and sought out Senusert.

He found him in one of the small state chambers consulting with Inpy, the architect. The old man was proudly explaining the secret passages and traps built into the late king's pyramid to foil robbers. Ameni waited patiently by the door, studying his brother. What he saw shocked him. He had been away just over two weeks, and already his twin had taken on some of the lines of worry and fatigue that had marked their father's face. But when the young king looked up, the shadows vanished.

"Ameni! I knew Ankhrekhu would find you." He rushed

over and hugged his brother, then waved a hand of dismissal to the architect. "Leave us now."

"Did you see that?" Senusert said when Inpy had gone. "That's the part I can't get used to. I tell people to do something, and they do it."

"That's what comes of being a god."

His brother smiled wryly. "Well, if having folks bow and scrape is the only advantage, I'd say divinity is overrated."

"I was wondering about that. I mean . . . did you feel anything?"

"When Father died?" They looked at each other, but said nothing. Their grief was too perfectly shared to need words. Senusert turned and walked to a couch. With its golden lion-shaped supports, it had been their father's favorite. He gestured for his brother to join him. "No, I felt nothing special. I was so miserable and so tired by then, I guess I was just numb."

Of course, Ameni thought. His twin had been here and hardly needed to be hit over the head with a divine vision. And when he himself had been, he had not understood it. Some priest he'd make.

Absently Senusert fingered his gold amulet. "This is all so hard, Ameni. It's not just that I'm not ready, it's that I don't know if I'll ever be ready. I don't mean for grand things like leading the army. It's the everyday things: planning the buildings and irrigation projects, worrying about grain supplies and about whether some noble in the south is abusing his tenants. In the end, the king is responsible for every person in Egypt. Ameni, if there's one thing I've learned already, it's that you should offer thanks to those gods who held *you* back at the time of our birth."

Ameni laughed. "I've been doing that for years."

"In that case," Senusert said, smiling, "I'll be quick about producing heirs so you'll never have to face this."

"You're so anxious to marry Merseger?"

His brother groaned. "That's the worst duty of all. I don't care what priests say about royal bloodlines. Kings shouldn't have to marry their sisters—at least not a sister like that! Already she's bossing people around like the 'Great Queen.' But surely somewhere in this kingdom I can find someone to be as devoted to me as Neferhent is to you."

Ameni blushed and changed the subject.

The two talked late into the night. Torches were lit and servants brought in plates of fruit, cakes, and cheese. In the end, Ameni felt closer to his twin than he had in many years.

The next morning after a short and troubled sleep, Ameni awoke to find Ankhrekhu standing by his bed. "Sorry to disturb you, your highness, but yesterday I neglected to say that you and I need to leave for Abydos today."

He sat up groggily. "Abydos? But I just got back to the palace. Surely I'm needed here."

"True, but you are needed in Abydos even more. You have been trained as a priest of Osiris. But you must be fully initiated in the god's mysteries, and in his main temple, if you are to fulfill your duties from now on."

"But how long will that take, with the travel and all? Surely I have to be back for my father's burial."

"Don't worry, it is essential that this be completed before then."

"Abydos. The last time I was there, I decided it was the gloomiest temple I'd ever seen. Wouldn't some little shrine to Osiris do? No, don't answer that. When must we leave?"

"This morning."

"What?"

"I've already told the others you're leaving. Best to get ready now and not waste any time in leave-taking. You had many glad greetings yesterday, and those are best."

By sunset that day, the priest and his royal pupil were well on their way up the Nile. The sails billowing with north wind were supplemented by straining oars.

Ameni always enjoyed river trips: the slowly passing panorama of cliffs and fields, temples and palm trees, and the constant colorful activity in the villages and towns and on the busy river. But this time as he watched, he kept wondering about the people that he passed. Singing drunks, perhaps, or greedy mortuary priests, conniving thieves, worried old women, hardworking scribes, or the loving families of fishermen. And how many more types that he had never met? But he would meet them, and many others. He'd go adventuring yet. Once his father was buried and his brother officially on the throne, then he'd take up his own life again. All of Ankhrekhu's preaching about duty would not change that.

After several days their boat moored at Abydos, and the travelers made their way up from the busy riverside toward the great temple of the god Osiris. Ameni found it every bit as huge and gloomy as he remembered. He and Ankhrekhu were greeted under the towering entry pylons by two other priests. One was as small and wizened as a dry, dead bird, while the other, even with his shaven head, seemed far too young and good-natured to be a convincing priest of Osiris. With the ancient priest in front and the other two on either side of the prince, they advanced down the vast hall, the tops of its gigantic columns lost in purple shadows.

Enclosed by massive stone walls, the dim air was cold and clouded with incense. From some side chapel came the jingling of sistrums and the monotonous chanting of priests.

Monumental paintings of processing gods glowered down at them from all sides. Ameni wished he were somewhere else. Anywhere else.

They passed through the first hall and into another and another. They ought at least to have more torches in the place, Ameni thought. The statues and paintings would seem less threatening if they weren't looming half-seen in shadow. Of course, they were probably meant to seem threatening. They certainly succeeded.

Finally they came to a small golden door, with a guardian priest before it. The high priest rasped out a singsong phrase, and the guard threw back a bolt. The four stepped inside, and the door closed heavily behind them.

The Holiest of Holies. Ameni had never been this far, this close to the presence of the god. Gold glinted everywhere in the fluttering light of wall torches. Magnificent paintings of gods and kings adorned the walls, their vibrant colors dimmed by the sweet blue clouds of incense that filled the air. In the midst of the room stood a golden shrine, its doors flung open. Standing inside was the god, the golden statue of the mummified Osiris. It was draped with rich fabric and jewelry, and a cake of incense burned steadily before it.

The four mortals bowed to their god, then Ankhrekhu turned and bowed to his prince. "Amenemhat, son of the Good God, the Osiris, Senusert II, may he live forever; it is for you to speak the words of praise to the god."

Ameni's heart sank like a stone. He had learned endless prayers and praises to many gods. But could he remember any of them now? He closed his eyes trying to recall hieroglyphs marching across papyrus, the papyrus with prayers to Osiris.

He bowed low before the statue, then straightened, opened his mouth, and hoped the right words would come out.

"Homage to thee, great Osiris, King of Eternity, Lord of Everlastings, the God of Gods, the King of Kings, the Governor of the World, whose forms are manifold, whose existence is everlasting.

"Thy name is established in the mouths of men, thou art the substance of the Two Lands, the celestial oceans rise from thee, thou sendeth forth the north wind at eventide, and the great doors of the sky open themselves before thee. The imperishable stars are obedient unto thee, and the stars that never set are thy throne. The uttermost parts of the earth bow down before thee, and all Egypt offers thanksgiving unto thee. Gracious is thy face and beloved by him that sees it. Thy fear is set in all the lands by reason of thy perfect love."

Again Ameni bowed his head. There was more, but that was all that came, and it seemed right. He waited in silence, though he was not sure for what. Not an answer, certainly. But an answer came. Not from the statue but from the mouth of the high priest.

The voice was not the reedy cackle Ameni had heard there earlier. It was rich and deep and echoing, like a voice carried over water.

"Greetings, Son of Osiris, the Living Horus, Lord of the Two Lands, Kakure, Son of the Sun, Amenemhat, Living Forever. May your works prosper and your duties be fulfilled, from everlasting to everlasting."

Ameni stared at the old man. His face, which had become serenely calm, now shriveled again into its leathery creases. The prince turned and whispered to Ankhrekhu.

"Isn't there some mistake? Those are the titles of a king. I'm only the son of a king and the brother to one."

His tutor took a long deep breath and looked him in the eye. "You are the son of a king—his *eldest* son. It was you who

71

were born first, not your twin. I placed the amulets about your necks but told their true meaning to none but those in this room.

"Amenemhat, it is you who are the Living Horus, the Son of Osiris, the right born King of Egypt."

EIGHT

Ameni did not remember sitting down. But the young priest had brought up a gilded chair, and he found himself sitting in it.

"Why?" he asked at last.

Ankhrekhu looked down at him, his usual worried face touched with relief and certainty. "Because the gods need you. Because the gods need one of their own—a god who can do their work in this world in places and times where they may not hold sway.

"Think, your majesty. Since your youngest years you have studied the ways of the gods, and you have learned the prescribed ways for men to share in the immortality of those gods, to live forever in the otherworld. In all that study, have you seen no weak link in that chain?"

Ameni only looked more confused.

Frowning slightly, the priest continued. "Then think of your own father whose journey to the afterworld is close at hand. For seventy days he will be prepared for burial. His body will be bathed in natron, his organs placed in exquisite jars of alabaster. He will be annointed with precious oils and wrapped in bandages of the finest linen along with every protective charm. Then his body will be draped in gold and jewels and placed in a coffin on the insides of which are carefully written all the instructions needed to safely reach the throne room of Osiris, all the formulas he need know and all the names he need recite.

"And then when he is finally placed in the tomb, beside him will go all things needful for a pleasant life in the afterworld: clothing and jewelry, his game boards and hunting weapons. Even a boat will be there and figures of servants to work for him and do his bidding. Food and wine will be placed there to sustain his soul, and land will be endowed so that offerings can be made to him for all eternity.

"But how long, Ameni, how long will eternity last? All these things are needful to sustain his soul. That we have been taught. Yet how will that soul fare in even a few hundred years?"

Ameni's face clouded, remembering the plundered, crumbling pyramids of the great kings of the past. "Not well," he whispered.

"No, not well," the priest replied. "Thieves will no doubt have foiled all of Inpy's clever traps, the tomb will be bare of treasure, the body despoiled and left to decay. The endowed land will have somehow found other uses, and the mortuary offerings will have been forgotten. Later kings will have used the very stones of his pyramid for their own buildings.

"And if this is so with kings, how much more fragile is the immortality of common folk? People who believed in our faith and lived their lives by its precepts so that in the final judgment their souls would balance against the feather of rightness and be entitled to life eternal? They saved up their wealth against their deaths, and their grieving families scrimped to place fine burial offerings in their tombs. In even a few years will not these unguarded tombs also be plundered and the hopes for immortality of those who lie there be scattered like their bones upon the sand?"

Ameni was thinking. He was remembering the local noble, Ptahotep, whose crumbling temple had sheltered him. How long would his own poor offering of three dates sustain that neglected soul? And he thought too of the old woman whose son and grandson would never even receive proper burial. They might have led good, worthy lives, but what chance had they even to see the afterworld?

He looked up, his face troubled with sudden doubt. "But all those people had faith, they believed in the promises of the gods. What . . . what are you saying?"

"I am saying that their faith should not be betrayed. Their belief that certain things are needed for eternal life means that denial of those things places their eternal lives in jeopardy. The gods know this. Osiris, lord of the otherworld is troubled by it. So the gods have decreed that something be done to save the souls of all those who in times past or to come live and die by our faith."

Ameni stood up and paced across the room, pausing to trace a finger unthinkingly along an incised inscription. "But what can possibly be done? Is there any way to save them—to save any of us?"

"With guidance from the gods and employment of all our powers and spells, we priests of Osiris have divined a way. Offerings were prepared, offerings of all things needful for sustaining souls in the afterworld. Then through great and powerful magic these things were compressed and refined until their essence is now contained in two jars. Potent and mysterious, this essence of life-sustaining offerings is held in two alabaster jars, sealed forever. They synthesize the eternal hope of all believers, male and female, whether past, present, or to come. They will be hidden away most carefully. And as long as they are safe, as long as they remain in Egypt, then the eternity they promise is secure."

Ameni frowned. "Yes, but you said yourself, eternity is a long time. Suppose in hundreds or thousands of years, those urns are found? Suppose some robbers find them or some foreign people conquer the land and carry them off as booty? Then our eternity will be lost again."

"Indeed, we have thought of that. In time, change threatens all things. That is why there must be a guardian. A guardian with the strengths of a god but at the same time one who can walk and work among men. And there is only one such in the world at any time, the Living Horus, the true king."

Ameni felt a tingle of alarm at the back of his skull. "But that's no good, really. If these things are destroyed or carried off, it will likely be in some time where there is no strong pharaoh. There have been times of disorder like that before."

"Of course. That is why this guardian must remain with the urns. As a god himself, the gods will preserve his body and his life, even in the tomb, until such time as he may need to perform his divine duties, his position as the Living Horus restored."

Now alarm was jangling through Ameni's whole body. He struggled to control his trembling.

"It's me, isn't it? It's me you want to wall up in a tomb with a couple of pots—to stay there till the gods know when, maybe forever."

"It is your duty. It is what you have been trained for all your life. You are skilled at weapons and possess quickness of thought. You know the ways of the gods and the ways and languages of foreign peoples. If the land has been overrun with invaders, the Sea People perhaps or even the Hittites, you could speak with them. And you are a god. If in days to come belief in the gods has waned and the gods care little for mankind, they will still help one of their own."

"But my life! You are asking me to give up my life, everything I've ever hoped to do!"

"In order to preserve the eternal life of everyone you love, of everyone who has ever believed in the gods of this land or ever will. It is a heavy duty, but an inescapable one."

Ameni slumped again into the chair, shaken and silent. The demands of duty he had sensed earlier were now hammering at him like mallets. He felt crushed under their blows.

"When?" he whispered at last.

"Immediately."

Without willing it, he flinched, as if from another blow.

Ankhrekhu's face softened, almost with pain. "We hadn't planned it like this, believe me, Ameni. It would have been better if you could have matured, if you could have prepared more. But now there is no time. You must begin your guardianship before your father is buried and your brother officiates as king."

"But . . . but surely I should be there then."

"Your majesty, you cannot be. If the priests were to perform the ceremonies of kingship for someone who is in fact not the Living Horus, it would anger the gods. Great havoc might be wreaked upon the land. No, you are the Living God, and in that state you must be turned over to the other gods, taken out of this world, not to their own but to a place between the two. There you must wait as the hawk waits in the shell, while the god's living incarnation passes to your brother and to those who follow him, so that his kingship and those after it may be valid. You will not be dead; embalmers must never touch you, for you may need to act again as Living Horus. I will report an accident in which you died and your body was lost. But you must not return to Itowe—not in this lifetime."

For a long while Ameni sat in silence, looking blankly at the crystal amulet clutched in his hand. Ankhrekhu stepped beside him and placed a hand on his shoulder.

"Ameni, this grieves me deeply. Every year you have become more like a son than a pupil to me. I dreaded this day and hoped to see it postponed for a long while yet." Ameni said nothing. There seemed nothing to say. Sadly the priest continued. "Come then, I will answer more questions if you have them. But you should rest. We must leave here early tomorrow."

Ameni had no more questions. His brain couldn't form any. He slept that night in a priest's room and was awakened before dawn, dressed and given a gray hooded robe. The others, similarly robed, spirited him out of the temple and down to the river, its wide, calm surface still shrouded in morning mist. The dockside, which later in the day would throng with pilgrams to the temple of Osiris, was now deserted and eerily quiet.

The golden sun rose to find them out on the river. Their boat was swift and unadorned, manned by a crew loyal to the temple but who had no idea of their fourth passenger's identity. He sat under a fringed canopy in silent brooding. The food and wine brought him were good, but he scarcely noticed. He ate mechanically, and slept, and listlessly watched the banks of Upper Egypt as they slid by. He spoke very little to anyone.

For a time they sailed south, but when the great river took an eastward loop and the north wind no longer aided them, the striped sails were furled and the oars taken up.

As always, the river and its banks were alive with activity. Fishing boats, freight barges, and pleasure craft slid by them. Temples and fields and bustling villages passed on the banks. But Ameni paid little attention. What was the point in watching the life around him? He was dead anyway. This might as well be his funerary barge. What a contrast to the way life and travel had seemed just a few days earlier. And that fact set up a tiny wave of concern in his mind. Sluggishly it grew.

As Ankhrekhu was bringing a midday meal, Ameni placed a listless hand over his cup. "You've put something in the wine. Or is it the food?"

His tutor looked at him searchingly a moment, then lowered his gaze. "The wine. The others thought you needed something to make this ordeal easier for you. But I rather think it would be better if your mind were clear. You're strong enough to do what is needed. What do you say?"

For answer, Ameni simply kept his hand over the cup.

His gold armlets flashed in the sun as Ankhrekhu hurled

the wine jug over the side. The startled rowers watched it gurgle and sink into the blue-green water. "I'll fetch another vintage."

By the time the boat docked, Ameni was seeing the world differently. Everything was sharp again, blooming with color and life. His heavy lethargy was replaced by tingling anxiety and slowly growing dread. He had to admit that this was not altogether an improvement. But if this was the last adventure open to him, he ought at least to be aware of it.

The town was a sizable one with gleaming stone temples and two-story houses of whitewashed brick. Its dockside was alive with noise and activity. The great eastern caravan route ended here, and the town also served as port for the stone quarries set back in the wadis.

On the dock nearby, several large blocks of hard red stone were being loaded onto a barge amid shouted instructions from foremen and onlookers. Despite himself, Ameni watched with interest. These were probably intended for some royal building project that his father had begun and his brother now must finish. Ameni shook his head. And here he used to think that supervising building projects was the most onerous duty of a true king.

Ankhrekhu urged him to hurry, and reluctantly he left the bustling dock and mounted one of the donkeys that the priests had readied. Soon the lively sounds of the riverside had dropped behind and been replaced by a rasping hot wind and the oppressive silence of the eastern desert. The glare off sand and rock was intense, and despite his protective eye paint, Ameni closed his eyes and let the donkey choose its own route forward.

With his reviving awareness and fear had also come renewed curiosity. Finally, although he knew an answer would bring him no comfort, he urged his donkey up beside Ankhrekhu's.

"Where is it exactly that we are heading? I'd have thought you would have chosen a spot nearer the Nile."

"The idea was to avoid places a robber might look. The west bank normally contains tombs, so we couldn't go there. In fact anyplace by the river near good farmland might in the future become a village. If we actually dug anywhere, we would call attention to ourselves; so instead we are using an abandoned quarry as a tomb. The quarry hole we chose was played out some years ago, but it's near others still in use, so our occasional activities in the area have not been noticed."

Ameni tried to be dispassionate, as his father had always seemed when inspecting the work on his own pyramid, "A tomb, you say?"

Tightness flickered across Ankhrekhu's face. "Sorry. Perhaps treasury or guardroom would be a better choice of words. Over the years we have prepared it, little by little. All is now in readiness."

Except for me, Ameni thought. He wasn't ready to walk out of the world into his tomb—maybe never to leave it. Wasn't there some other way to insure his people's immortality? If he was the Living God, what about the *Living* part? Shouldn't he be allowed some of that first?

They rode on, Ameni's thoughts circling between panicky objections and irrefutable explanations. Overhead in the sharp blue sky, a pair of hawks also circled, but their movement had the certainty of accepted purpose.

They camped for the night in a side wadi not far from the main route. Avoiding the tumbled rocks for fear of snakes and scorpions, they spread bedrolls on the open ground.

Feeling every lump and pebble beneath him, Ameni lay tense and sleepless while the others breathed softly beside him.

Slowly a great full moon cleared the dark cliffs above him, glowing pure and white like a lamp of living alabaster. But its beauty and peace could not seem to quiet his mind. Perhaps they should have camped in the rocks. Wouldn't death by snakebite be preferable to this? The timing and meaning of such a death was clearly a decision of the gods. But this? As much as he loved and respected Ankhrekhu, how could he be sure the priest had interpreted the gods' will correctly? Was this really his unquestionable duty?

Surely the gods would not inflict punishment on Egypt if through innocent mistake people crowned a king who by a few moments was not actually the eldest royal son. And surely the gods could not object if he chose to live a while longer, if he passed a few years yet among fisherfolk or farmers or travelers to distant lands. How did he know he should not? The gods had given *him* no sign of their intentions for him. Perhaps they did not want their fellow god, the Living Horus, entombed like this. Perhaps it was *not* his duty.

Almost before he had realized it, he had slipped from his blanket and was putting on his sandals. He wouldn't take a donkey, they made too much noise. Besides it would be safer if he cut to the river through the mountains rather than back down the wadi. There would be less likelihood of their finding him and winning him back with persuasive talk of divine duty.

Creeping like a cat to the saddlebags, he shouldered a water flask and a bag of bread and hard cheese, then headed to the base of a cliff. A moment's search showed him a trail that wild goats had etched up into the rocks. Anxiously he began climbing.

Except for his own whispered passage, the night was quiet. Even the wind had stilled, as if the world were holding its breath. The mosaic of silver moonlight and sharp black shadows added to the strangeness. The world seemed not less real, but different, as if he had moved into another world, a world peopled by gods and spirits perhaps, one oddly alien to his own.

Suddenly the waiting stillness was pierced by a high shivering wail. He stopped dead, fear quivering through him as the cry twice repeated itself. A jackal. Only a jackal, a wild dog of the night. They were no danger. Not ordinary jackals.

He moved on, but the fear followed him. Jackals were not ordinary, not always. They were also the animals sacred to Anubis, guardian of the gods, divine guide of souls.

Faster and faster he hurried over the narrow hoof-pricked trail, crazily careering through white moonlight and inky black shadows. In the rocky gorge around him, fear and tension built in the air as if from a waiting storm.

Something stood before him on the path. He stopped, and it almost seemed that his heart stopped as well. The jackal was huge and black. Its lean dog shape, its fine pricked ears, were edged about with silver moonlight. But its eyes glowed from within. They looked directly at him.

Then the creature threw back its head, and its wailing cry tore into him, pouring molten fear into the depth of his bones. With a whimper he sank to his knees. After an eternity of sound, the echoes thinned, fading finally from the reverberating cliffs. Fearfully Ameni looked up. The creature was gone.

He lowered one hand to steady himself. It touched nothing. He looked down. Concealed in the black shadow of a rock stretched a deep bottomless cleft, cutting across his path maybe three feet wide. A nimble goat on this route could have leaped it easily, but in his wild flight, he had been just a step from plummeting into it. Had it not been for the jackal . . .

He shivered from head to toe. Anubis, guide and guardian of the gods. Even now, fleeing from his own divine duty, his life had been spared. Had he wanted a sign?

Leaning back against a rock, he finally let the night's calm seep into him. The fever of fear had broken. He might wish to have been born another, to another's duties. But that could not be. He was who he was. The Living Horus, Lord of the Two Lands, Kakure Amenemhat.

Resolutely he stood up and walked back the way he had come, walked back to whatever the gods asked of him.

NINE

 Slowly Lorna stepped into the tomb. Thoughts of Howard Carter finding Tutankhamon vanished in the wonders of her own discovery. Her sweeping flashlight showed white plastered walls adorned with gods. Their brightly painted figures marched in eternal majesty, in cold daunting calm.

With difficulty she drew her light from them and let it play over the huge sarcophagus filling the center of the room. It was carved from a solid block of alabaster, glowing a pale pinkish-gold in her light. At its head set in niches in the wall were two graceful urns, maybe ten inches high, made of the same vibrant stone. On the floor beside the sarcophagus were ranged a number of wonderfully ornamented chests, ebony set with bits of ivory and gold, or paler wood laid over with gold leaf and enamel. Beside them stood a large pottery wine jar and baskets that must once have held food.

Impatiently her father and the others crowded behind her, asking what she saw. She had no words to convey it, so reluctantly she stepped aside. That first magical moment of discovery had passed, but she knew it would be part of her for the rest of her life.

The days and weeks that followed were consumed with exciting activity, and the best part, from Lorna's point of view, was that there was no more talk of her returning to England for the spring term. Eventually her father got around to sending her school a telegram saying she'd be back some time during the summer and could they please arrange some makeup tutoring.

Basic excavation continued on the village site, but most effort now concentrated on the tomb. The hole in the hillside was enlarged, ladders installed, and photographic equipment brought in. Everything was photographed, then the smaller items were carefully removed to the work tents. One of the chests proved to be filled with fine linen clothing, and another with jewelry of such richness and beauty that Lorna could scarcely bring herself to touch it even when it was laid out for cataloging. In a third chest lay a bronze dagger with a gold hilt, a bow and quiver of arrows, and several carved throwing sticks. Everything seemed almost perfectly preserved, except that the food in the baskets had shriveled into hard, dry lumps and the wine had long ago evaporated.

Eventually everything had been removed from the stone

chamber except the sarcophagus itself. Dr. Padgett was examining this one afternoon when Lorna joined him.

"You know, Lorna," he said running his fingers over the smooth, pale stone, "we keep referring to this as a sarcophagus. But I don't see how it can be. Look, there's simply no crack, no seam. It's shaped like a sarcophagus, but I don't think there's a top and bottom. There can't be a mummy inside. It's just one solid piece of stone."

"But all the other things look like burial goods."

"Yes, to a certain extent. The jewelry and clothes certainly, and the food. But there isn't the variety of things that usually accompanies a dead person, not someone of this obvious rank at least. One of the chests carries the cartouche of King Senusert II, so the deceased must have been one of his relatives or courtiers.

"And where are the four canopic jars holding the mummy's internal organs? Those two urns from the niches are solid stone; they can't be opened any more than can this sarcophagus."

"So you don't think this is a tomb?"

"Not one with a body, anyway. It's probably a cenotaph, a substitute burial for some important person who died somewhere else. Though why they'd choose a godforsaken place like this, I don't know."

"Hmm." Lorna shifted her eyes to the walls now lit with a battery of lights hooked to a humming portable generator. "Well, maybe that explains why the wall paintings are so odd. You said yourself they don't look like the usual tomb stuff."

"No they don't. There ought to be scenes of the deceased enjoying the afterlife or of Anubis guiding his soul into the judgment hall of Osiris. Now at the end there, we do have

Anubis and Osiris and the scales, and the Devourer squatting there waiting to gobble up any failed souls. But there's no soul being weighed against the Feather of Rightness. There's just Horus and Isis presenting two vases. It's wonderful work, but I really don't understand it."

Lorna didn't either. It was too bad there was no mummy. But at least those awful sensational newspapers she saw whenever she was in England wouldn't be badgering them for stories about curses. And the very absence of a mummy added to the mystery, which in its own way made things even more exciting. They'd figure it out in the end, she was sure.

In the meantime, she enjoyed helping record the finds and packing them carefully for their trip downriver to the association's Cairo institute. She did wish there were more inscriptions to read. Other than the one cartouche of Senusert II, there were only the names of each god inscribed above its painted figure and endless repetitions of the ankh sign for eternal life. She wished ancient peoples had been more thoughtful of future archaeologists. Obviously something interesting had happened here, and they hadn't recorded a word about it. A few "succinct explanatory paragraphs," as her English teacher said, would have been quite nice.

Finally the day arrived when everything was ready for the trip north. The enormous fake sarcophagus weighed down the back of one truck, while the other treasures, packed in wooden crates, were stowed in a second.

Despite her pleas for further delay, Lorna was traveling north as well. Her father was suffering from renewed guilt about ignoring his daughter's education. He was determined she make up for her spring in Egypt by being tutored in England during the summer, then staying through the term until next winter break.

Lorna was distressed, but knew she could only stretch her luck so far. It had been a glorious spring. And she still had some time ahead of her at their Cairo apartment above the institute. Abdul Rahman, the association's secretary, would be there, of course, but since she was supposed to stay there only a short time, she probably wouldn't have to put up with servants. Basically she'd have the place to herself, with its crowded museum rooms and lovely walled garden. Her father would be staying at the excavation for a while yet, so she'd stretch her stay in Cairo as long as she possibly could.

That proved fairly easy. Once she and the finds had completed their river trip and arrived at the institute, everything had to be unpacked and displayed so that representatives of the Cairo Museum could examine them. The association worked under a standard agreement that the unique items would remain in Egypt, while those of which there were several roughly similar examples would be divided, with half going to the association's London institute.

Abdul Rahman usually handled that end of things, but since Lorna was familiar with these particular items, he welcomed her help. Once the Egyptian authorities had made their selections, everything had to be properly packed again, some for trucking to the Cairo Museum and some for sending by air to London. It was a busy few weeks, and Lorna relished every delaying minute.

The British items, being fewer and smaller, were packed up first. Finally they were stowed in the association's truck, and Abdul Rahman drove them off to the airport. That afternoon, Lorna, not wanting to see airports any sooner than she had to, stayed in her room and brooded.

She brooded about her looming exile, about boring school subjects, inflexible teachers, and having to "learn to get along with people" she couldn't stand. She brooded about not having any friends, and when the niggling thought intruded that this could be her own fault, she thrust it aside as being disruptive to her splendid brooding.

It was a fine day for brooding. All afternoon the usually clear blue sky had been clouding over. The air felt heavy and threatening, giving her a dull headache. Egypt seldom had major thunder storms, but Lorna guessed they were in for one now. Thunder rumbled distantly over the city. Through her window, she could see lightning shimmering ominously in the western sky, eerily silhouetting the skyline of minarets and skyscrapers.

Finally it became too exciting. She had to get up from her bed and watch at the window. Presumably the flight with the antiquities would get off all right; surely they wouldn't let the plane fly if the weather were too dangerous. But Abdul Rahman would not be back soon. Tomorrow was a holiday, and he was spending the day with his parents in one of Cairo's suburbs, driving there directly from the airport instead of returning to his apartment in the front of the institute. That was fine by Lorna. She wasn't afraid. This place had more locks on it than a bank, and solitude gives brooding more scope.

The bushes and palm trees in the garden below were now thrashing about in a violent wind. The sky glowed with an ominous green cast. Closer now, lightning jabbed down in alarming forks, followed quickly by sharp booming thunder. Suddenly the world went white and was filled with sound. The thunderous crack seemed to shake the building to its foundations. Then the light faded, and when her ears stopped ringing, thunder was rumbling only in the distance.

Lorna was shaken. She had never been so close to a lightning strike before. It was a wonder the concussion hadn't broken all the glass in the windows.

Break the glass. It could, couldn't it? Alarmed she sped downstairs heading for the room with the new finds. Most had been left on the table ready to pack for the museum. But the house had shaken so, some could have toppled off and broken.

Heart racing, she skidded into the room, afraid of what she would find. All seemed well. The beautiful alabaster urn, the one that Cairo had chosen to keep, had shifted but hadn't toppled over. Gratefully she placed it in a box, tucking some paper around it. There might be more thunder.

She loved the feel of that stone, particularly the great block of it that had been used for the fake sarcophagus. Stepping over to it now, she rubbed an appreciative hand over its silky surface. Then she stopped, puzzled. Had she felt a crack?

She looked closely. Yes, there was definitely a faint line in the stone. That concussion had broken something. This was terrible! What would the museum think? What would her father think?

Anxiously she examined the crack. The blast must have jolted some natural flaw in the stone, for the line looked very regular. In fact, it seemed to run all the way around, a few inches from the top.

An exciting thought sprang at her. Could it . . . could it just possibly be a lid? Maybe this wasn't a solid piece of stone after all. Maybe over the centuries, over the millennia, the lid had almost fused with the base. And the thunder had cracked it loose.

A stone lid, she knew, could be very heavy. But instinctively she placed her hands against it and gave a little shove. She felt movement. This thing might open!

But she mustn't do this on her own. She should wait until Abdul Rahman got back, day after tomorrow. Or maybe she should telegraph her father or phone somebody at the Cairo Museum. Maybe it was too heavy for her anyway.

Against all her better judgment, she gave the top a harder shove. The joint was smoothly crafted, and with scarcely a jerk, the lid slid halfway off. Alarmed, she grabbed for it so it wouldn't slide off and break. Cautiously she lowered the lid over the edge until it rested between the base and the wall. Only then did she allow herself to look inside.

She gasped. She had never been so close to fainting in her life. Then she looked closer and almost laughed at herself. What at first had seemed to be a person swathed in shawls, was clearly only a wax figure. Or more likely it was a wax coating over a bandaged mummy, skillfully painted to look lifelike.

It certainly did that. A fine linen shroud was draped over the body of the mummy, but the head was uncovered and painted so delicately that the soft-looking surface gave the illusion of real skin. Inside the wax and the enshrouding bandages, the real mummy had probably shrunken to a leathery gnomelike figure. But the outer image was still as the artist had left it four thousand years earlier.

It had the face of a boy, a boy she realized who might have been her own age. And somehow he looked a little familiar. Did she know someone like him? Maybe one of the Egyptians helping on the dig? No one she knew, however, would wear a headcloth in that ancient Egyptian fashion. A small crystal amulet hung at the boy's throat, and through the sheer linen she could see hands crossed over his bare chest, holding a crook and flail of gold and lapis lazuli.

That was very odd. Those were royal symbols, a king's

symbols. Perplexed, she stepped back. Then she noticed the hieroglyphics running around the inside of the sarcophagus lid. They were probably the usual coffin text, a guidebook for the soul of the dead so it could avoid the monsters and lakes of fire and remember all the instructions for getting to the afterworld. Still, the inscriptions might include a name or something.

Leaning over the open sarcophagus, she began to read the text. She read aloud, loving as always the melodious sounds of the long-dead language. Slowly she recited line after line; but this was not the usual coffin text, the stuff used in every primer on how to read ancient Egyptian. It was instead a long enumeration of the various gods, and a request that they watch over their fellow god that he might watch over eternity. Very odd.

Then excitedly her eyes jumped ahead several lines. There was a name. More than just a name, it was a *royal* name, written in two encircling cartouches. She read it carefully several times. "Kakure Amenemhat." A Twelfth-Dynasty king, surely. They were all named Amenemhat or Senusert. But which was this? She had learned all the king lists once, and something seemed a little wrong about this name. Well, it could be checked easily enough. There was a library just down the hall.

Quickly she ran to the library, flicked on the light and scanned the shelves. Pulling out the book she needed, she plunked it onto the table and flipped to the king lists in the back. As she'd thought, Kakure was the throne name of a Senusert, not an Amenemhat. It was Senusert III, successor to the king whose cartouche had been on that little chest. But who could this boy have been then?

She flipped back to the chapter on the Twelfth Dynasty.

Suddenly she knew why the figure had seemed so familiar. Before her was a photograph of a statue she had seen many times in the British Museum. Senusert III. It looked almost identical to the figure lying in the other room, except that the man shown in the statue was clearly older and more care-worn. But there were the same big ears, the strong chin, the high cheekbones. The mouth turned down at the corners in the same little frown, and there was even an identical amulet on the chest. Surely these two must have been related!

Excited almost beyond bearing, she grabbed up the book and ran back into the other room. Where she slid to an incredulous halt. The sarcophagus was empty.

TEN

His memory was of time. Time as a pure thing. Not as an empty duration between one event and another, but as a substance in itself, like an endlessly flowing river. It carried him with it, submerged in the sensation and music of its motion, never ceasing and never causing him to want or to remember anything more.

Other memories moved with him, but like scraps caught in the same eddy. Images of entering the rock-hewn tomb, of invoking the gods, of chanting and incense, and of laying himself in the stone carved to receive him. Images of the gods, too, stayed with him, shadowy distant images, more a presence than a vision. He knew their names and forms yet his sense of them was less of separate beings than of parts of a single awareness, facets of an endless caring.

Into this constant stream of time, there suddenly came a moment. Something shattered the absence of things. A noise, a shock, and he was floating on time's surface, no longer carried within it.

Other noises came to his ears, words in his own language. Badly spoken and stumbled over, yet soft and earnest. A young girl's voice. A foreign voice.

He wanted to see now as well as hear. Slowly his body remembered, and his eyelids raised, ever so slightly. Caution held him. He knew nothing of how things might be.

Through a fringe of dark lashes, he saw the girl. Her hair was a color he had never imagined hair could be. It shimmered about her head like burnished bronze. Her skin was pale and dappled like leaf-shadowed sand, and her eyes were a strange blue-green, as if inlaid with faience.

She was speaking, leaning across him and reading the text on the sarcophagus lid. The soft sounds in her words were ill-chosen and misplaced, but he could catch the meaning. The voice stopped, seemed to skip, then spoke his name, his full name, several times. The girl stepped back, spoke words in another language as if to herself, then moved from his sight. He heard hurrying footsteps fading away.

He opened his eyes fully now and flexed sluggish hands and feet. Slowly he sat up, and the linen shroud slipped down into loose folds. The room around him was strange and disturbing.

Something about it was oddly foreign, alien. The light, harsh and white, came from a bar set in the ceiling. Its very alienness cast a vague shadow of fear.

There were objects on tables around him, some familiar, some with no names he could give them. Among them sat a box, and by some odd sense he knew what lay in it. An urn, a single urn. He understood now. The urns had been found, and one urn taken away. But whether he and this one had been taken from Egypt, or whether they had remained and the other urn been removed, he did not know.

But he needed to. He needed to know a good deal more about his current situation before he could begin fulfilling his duty.

He laid aside the crook and flail and weakly climbed out of the sarcophagus. Life slowly seeped back into his body. Unsteadily he walked to the table, reached into the box and pulled out the single urn that remained in his care. Then curiously he inspected the small cluttered room. It had only one door, which he dared not use for fear of meeting the girl. He did not know who she was or why she was here with him. Was it she or perhaps her people who had violated the tomb? Was she one of some foreign conquerors? Was he her captive? He'd better leave this place for a time until he had more answers.

He stepped to the windows. They were barred. And the openings were not really open but covered with thin, clear material like impossibly large sheets of rock crystal. The metal too was hard and unfamiliar. He found what must be a clasp and fumbled with it until it shifted. A gentle tug, and the whole window, bars and all, opened inward.

It was night outside, but still there was light in the street below. It came from poles holding more odd, flameless lights. The street itself seemed deserted, though there was a steady undercurrent of noise in the distance. He looked once more about the room, and spying several throwing sticks, grabbed an ebony one and stuck it into his waistband. Then holding the urn with one hand and the windowsill with the other, he slipped out the window and dropped lightly to the ground.

Now what? Best to walk about, mingle with people and learn where he was. Briskly Ameni strode up the street, but its very feel underfoot made him pause. The street and paved walk beside it were covered in strange sorts of stone. On the street it was black and unseamed.

He knelt to examine it when suddenly a frightful creature roared around a corner and bore down on him. It was large and dark and had two glowing eyes. With a yelp, he flung himself out of its path and stood flattened against a wall. Though he clutched at his throwing stick, he saw that it would be of little use if the demon turned on him. But it ignored him and rushed by, pursuing its own business.

He had barely stopped trembling when another monster came charging up the other way. This one also ignored him, and he watched intently as it passed. Perhaps it wasn't really an animal. He had glimpsed people sitting *inside* the thing. Some sort of vehicle then. But how was it propelled? Well, that didn't matter as long as the things weren't about to eat him.

He began walking again, but this time on the raised pathway. They might not eat him, but things that size could easily crush him and would probably enjoy doing it. Vehicles or not, they looked mean.

Two men in loose robes and curiously wound headclothes were walking along the pathway across the road from him. Pointing, they yelled something across to him. The words were totally foreign, but the tone he recognized. Derision. They repeated their phrase, then shrugged and walked on.

What was it they were deriding? Surely no one here could

recognize him. It must be his clothes, though they were deliberately ordinary looking—a simple kilt and headcloth, not even any gold thread. This must mean that he was in a foreign land, and they were making fun of him for being dressed like an Egyptian.

Anger bubbled up, but he fought it. Foreigners were barbarians, that was a given. But clearly he had to deal with them. He held the urn close to his side and trudged up the street.

Ahead, loud jarring music was pouring from an open door. Curious, he walked closer, and came near just as several men stumbled out laughing and singing drunkenly. They looked him over, one whooping with laughter and babbling something rude-sounding. The others joined in as the first made a drunken lunge his way.

He kicked out and sped across the street, narrowly missing another roaring vehicle, which hooted blaringly as it rushed past. One of the drunks half-heartedly pursued him, but he ran around a corner. And there he stopped abruptly, gaping in surprise and fear.

The street he had entered was alive with these vehicles swarming like huge insects. They filled the air with noise, smell and moving light. Despite the obviously late hour, people, outlandishly dressed, walked about and talked to one another in what he gradually realized were several foreign tongues. Lights were everywhere, colored lights and flashing lights. Some splayed over buildings like glowing snakes or shone through the stacked-up windows.

And these buildings were tall—tall and ugly. He saw several towering in the distance that were taller even than the Osiris temple at Abydos or that of Amun at Thebes.

While he stood and stared, he was also stared at. Men and

women in their absurd clothes stared as they walked by. Some pointed and laughed. Some spoke to him, then shrugged at his silence and walked on.

Suddenly Ameni knew he had never been so afraid in his life—not when the crocodile came for him, not when the jackal halted him on the mountain trail. Crocodiles and jackals, even the gods they represented, were familiar. But the alienness here was so complete, he could not even find words to describe it.

Some man wearing odd leg coverings was talking to him in an incomprehensible language. Ameni realized this only when the man reached out to touch the urn he held. Startled awake, he spat a curse at the other's profaning hands. Then clutching the urn, he turned and ran, though he ran not so much from one man as from everything.

He ran on and on through crowds and lights, noise and dangerous streets until finally he spied the dark mouth of an alley. Careening around its corner, he ran down it to another alley and another.

At last the panic ebbed. He leaned against a wall, panting and weak. This was no good. He had to stay calm, he had to think. Slumping to the trash-littered ground, he rested his head on his knees.

Everything around him was unbearably foreign, yet that did not necessarily mean he was in a foreign land. This certainly bore no resemblance to the foreign lands he had studied. And none of the languages he had heard now was anything like those he had studied.

The problem was not only one of place, but also one of time. He had no idea how much time had passed since he had been walled in that tomb, given to the care of the gods. It might have been hundreds of years, or hundreds of hundreds of years. By now foreign people could have conquored Egypt. He could be in their homeland now.

His thoughts were broken by a shuffling sound. Looking up, he saw a man in ragged robes slouching up the alley towards him. The look in the man's eyes was not derision, it was greed. This was a thief, like the ones he'd met in the palm grove. And like them, this man seemed intent on finding what things of value he might be carrying.

Several more steps. The ragged man smiled mirthlessly, then reached under his robes. Something flashed. A knife.

Ameni stood up, clutching the urn with one hand and drawing out his throwing stick with the other. The thief appraised the weapon, snorted and suddenly came for him with the knife. Ameni hurled his stick. The brittle wood shattered as it smashed against the turbaned head, but not before sending the man sprawling unconscious to the foul-smelling pavement.

Ameni stepped around his assailant, then stopped and bent over him. If he was going to learn anything of this place, he had to be less obviously Egyptian. A disguise was at hand.

Gingerly he pulled the robes off the man, shaking them out with distaste. The fellow was none too clean. Wrinkling his nose, he draped them over his own clothing, then took off the man's turban. But it was just too filthy. He dropped it like something dead, then removing his own headcloth, he re-wrapped it in some semblance of the other's style. Tying the urn in a fold of his new robe, he trotted up the alley.

Anonymous now, he walked on until the sky over the strange buildings began to lighten. Dawn found him on a walled embankment beside a great river. Foreign buildings rose on both banks, but in his heart he knew this was the Nile.

The discovery did not cheer him. As long as he might be in some foreign land, the strangeness seemed more bearable. But to know that his own land of Egypt had become like this. . . . The enormity of his plight finally hit him. Somewhere in a vast alien world he had to find that other small urn. And there was no one to turn to for help, for advice, for even a shred of familiarity. He was abandoned in a hostile sea, far more helpless than the shipwrecked sailor whose adventures had always thrilled him.

Slowly he walked away from the river, orphaned even by Father Nile. At this hour the streets were quieter, though hardly deserted. The rising sun gilded the tall buildings around him, but its once-familiar rays shed little comfort. He walked under an ornate building with a tall slender tower, and as he did so a call rang from it, calm and compelling, for all that the words were foreign.

Listlessly he looked at the carvings and colorful tiles that adorned the building. Rather attractive, in a barbaric sort of way. And there was something about it, something that spoke faintly of the gods.

With this dim spark of hope, he followed several other men inside, leaving his sandals, as they did, in a foyer. But when he stepped further inside, he knew he had been wrong. This place might indeed be sacred, but not to his gods. There were no statues of Amon or lion-headed Sekemet, no incense burning on an alter to Isis. The walls displayed no majestic paintings of Thoth or Horus, or Ptah, god of wisdom.

From a splendidly vaulted ceiling hung many filigree lamps. Men knelt on rich rugs, chanting in obvious prayer. He felt some divine presence here, but it was not his gods these men prayed to. Yet he almost knelt beside them. If he'd known how to pray to their gods, he might have been tempted. He so needed help.

Instead, retrieving his sandals, he slipped from the building and leaned dejectedly against its arched doorway. There was no point in going on like this. He was exiled, exhausted, and he just realized, incredibly hungry. And despite all his training, he couldn't speak one sentence to any of these people.

No, that wasn't totally true. There had been that girl. Her command of Egyptian had been far from perfect, but she had spoken his language. She might be someone he could learn things from. This one urn had been in that room; she might know where the other had gone.

Brightening suddenly, he knew what he had to do. He must return to that building and that girl. It would not be easy. He had paid little attention to the path of his flight. But he had been trained to find directions. And though this maze was far worse than any ever posed for him, the prize was greater.

More confident now, he stepped into the street, looking back at the building he had left. A shrine to foreign gods, yes. But surely his gods must have been lingering somewhere near. He had been given hope.

Not much hope, it was true. But to someone drowning in a foreign sea, any twig was worth grasping.

ELEVEN

In dismay, Lorna stared into the sarco-phagus. It was totally empty except for the crumpled linen and the crook and flail. She never should have opened it! Exposed to the air, the ancient mummy must simply have crumbled to dust. But no, that couldn't be. There wasn't anything left of it—not a speck of dust, not a scrap of wax. Surely something would have remained. And the linen shroud, every bit as old, was still intact.

Then it must have been stolen! Quickly she looked around. A window was swinging open. She ran to it. But these win-dows latched from the inside. She supposed somehow the storm could have jiggled the window open, and a passing thief could have crawled in and stolen the mummy. But why would he struggle to get an old dead body out of the narrow window when there was all this gold and jewelry lying about? At a quick glance, nothing else seemed to be missing.

She felt like crying, like jumping up and down and throwing a tantrum. She'd never felt so miserable in her life. By accident she'd made this wonderful discovery, then by carelessness she'd lost it. If she had never left the room, that thief could never have come in. If there was a thief, that is.

Could she somehow have imagined the mummy? Could she have opened an empty sarcophagus and then her disappointed imagination have made up a mummy? It had almost been too lifelike to be a real mummy, even a skillfully painted one.

But that was crazy. Just as crazy as the idea of a chance thief who preferred ancient corpses to gold. She couldn't possibly have imagined it. Or could she? Had she fallen asleep at some point and dreamed it? Or had it been some sort of weird hallucination? She had taken a couple of aspirin earlier for a headache. Suppose she'd mistakenly taken some other pills instead?

So, what had happened to Kakure Amenemhat? Had he crumbled away, been stolen, or simply been the figment of some weird drug trip? Should she call the police, write her father, or see a doctor? Nothing would do any good anyway. Real or imagined, the great discovery was gone.

Firmly she latched the window. She wouldn't do any of those things. She would go to bed. All this had given her another headache. But she was certainly staying away from that aspirin.

All night Lorna was pursued by guilt-ridden dreams, but

was never awakened enough to escape them. When she did wake in midmorning, she felt as if she'd been beaten from the inside. But she had made up her mind.

She would tell no one about the mummy. One way or another it was gone. She had opened a sarcophagus, and it had been empty except for an old sheet and a royal crook and flail. Perhaps her father had been right, after all. Perhaps it was a cenotaph for a hitherto unknown king, Kakure Amenemhat, who had died elsewhere. At least the coffin inscription was still there, and it did name that king. In any case, she didn't want to think about it anymore.

It was a good thing this was a holiday. Abdul Rahman was away, and the Cairo Museum people would not be working either. Put another night's sleep between herself and yesterday's bizarre events, and she'd be all right again. In the meantime, she'd stay out of that room and do something very unegyptological.

In the middle of the afternoon when she was well-immersed in a murder mystery, the doorbell chimed. Normally Abdul Rahman would be there to answer it. In fact, this might be he now. If he had forgotten his keys, it wouldn't be the first time. Annoyed, she put aside her novel and went downstairs. She opened the door and immediately wished she hadn't. She was, after all, a lone girl in a house full of valuable antiquities. She should first have looked through the spy hole, for this was some begger on the doorstep, or worse, maybe a thief. She started to close the door.

It had taken Ameni most of the day to find his way back to that building. This city was larger and more complex than any he'd ever imagined. He hadn't known there were this many people in the entire world, and they all seemed involved in bewildering, frightening, or noisy activities.

At one point he stumbled into a market, row after row of booths selling things, some familiar, some incomprehensible. He could have wandered there for hours except for two things: Merchants kept talking at him when he stopped to examine something; and he was sickeningly hungry.

There was food there aplenty, but he had no means to purchase any. He could have tried stealing, of course. He saw a couple of light-fingered children who did. But the last thing he wanted was to become embroiled with the authorities here. He didn't know anything about the current king, or what the laws were or the penalties for breaking them.

So he forged on through the city, getting turned around several times but always redirecting himself and working closer and closer to the building he sought, to the only person in all that clamor he had heard speak his language.

Finally, staggering with exhaustion and hunger, he found himself in a street he recognized. It led onto another, and there before him was the house. He turned to the door, then stopped. He didn't even know how to gain entry to these buildings.

He tried tapping on the door, waited, and nothing happened. Tried again—again nothing. Then he noticed a raised metal area at the side of the door. Perhaps if he knocked there, it would be louder. He tried and was startled by the gonging sound issuing from inside.

He felt a wave of panic. Suppose it was not she who answered the door? How would he ask for her? And suppose she proved to be an enemy to his mission? Well, he had no choice.

It was either learn something from her or give up his mission altogether.

Suddenly the door opened, and there she was. There was no mistaking that aurora of bronze hair. She stared at him, looking startled and perturbed, then began closing the door.

"Wait!" he said. "Great lady of the house, I need to speak with you."

Looking confused now, she replied in another language.

He tried again, speaking his own language slowly and clearly. "Please do not close me out. I am in great trouble and need to speak with someone."

Slowly her look of confusion changed into surprise. She frowned, then awkwardly framed a sentence he could understand. "You *speak* this language?"

"I speak many languages, but today I have heard none of them. I heard you speak mine though, last night."

Her expression changed again. A spark of recognition. She peered closely at his now smudged and dusty face. Unwinding the headcloth, he dropped it to the ground, then stepped out of the ragged robe until he was wearing only kilt, sandals, and amulet.

"Do you not remember me? Last night I was dressed like this.

She squealed and stepped back as if she had seen a snake. Her pale-flecked skin turned paler. Finally she seemed to recover herself, twitched a hand weakly and stammered, "Yes, please come in."

Gratefully he stepped into the cool shadowy hall, after first recovering the urn from the heap of rags. She looked at it in obvious surprise and said something in another language.

He shook his head but said, "I had to take this with me. I did not know I would be back."

Clearly she was having trouble understanding everything he said, but he was having trouble as well. She had most of the words and their proper order. But the soft sounds were wrong and in all the wrong places.

Slowly she walked around him and closed the door. Then she took a deep breath and said, "Are you Kakure Amenemhat?"

"Yes, I am."

Her face flickered with awe and a touch of relief. "But we know of no king by that name."

"I never ruled as king. My father did though, and so probably did my twin brother Senusert."

"Senusert III! Your twin brother. No wonder you look like him. We even have a little statue of him here."

"A statue of my brother?" He had caught that much. "May I . . . may I see it?"

"Yes, yes of course. In here."

In a nervous flutter she ran ahead, opened a door, led him down a hall, then opened another door. She touched something on a wall, and light filled the room.

The room was crammed from floor to ceiling with shelves and cases holding hundreds and hundreds of objects, all bespeaking the Egypt he knew. He saw crude water pots and delicate eating bowls. There were cases of jewelry, scarabs, and little servant figures from tombs. There were sections of carvings from buildings. Standing on the floor were the tops of columns, funerary offering-tables, and stone stelae with hieroglyphic inscriptions. And also there were statues. All sorts of statues: gods and kings, priests and noblemen, large and small, stone, metal, wood, and clay.

The girl quickly scanned the incongruously jumbled multitude, then pointed to a figure on a middle shelf.

"Here it is. I'd almost forgotten we had it."

Ameni stepped closer. The statue was of bronze, maybe ten inches high, of the sort usually given to temples. It showed a king kneeling with arms held before him, as if giving an offering. And the cold bronze face was Senusert's—or his own. Except it was older. The thin familiar face was seamed with weariness and care. Senusert had grown from boy to man, he had ruled a kingdom, shared its triumphs and dangers and daily routine. He had married, no doubt, and had children and finally died and been buried in some new stone pyramid. And all without Ameni, his own twin, who had shared his life since birth.

Suddenly the wall of purposeful duty Ameni had built around himself began to crumble. He was flooded with memories of people and of a world long turned to dust. His brother; his grieving mother; sweet, caring Neferhent; bouncy little Sithathor; and even wiley, conniving old Ankhrekhu. They had lived and died, and he would never know how. All their world was dead with them, and all its fishermen and scribes, farmers and priests. He was alone. A piece of wreckage washed onto an alien shore.

With one hand, Ameni touched the face of bronze, and the last of his defenses collapsed. Great sobs welled up within him. Raising trembling hands to his tear-streaked face, he slumped back against a table.

Distantly he felt the girl's hand on his shoulder and heard her speak in a foreign language and then in his own. "Come, sit down here." She guided him to a chair, and he collaped into it.

Trembling, he struggled to control his sobs. Finally he whispered, "I'm sorry. Please forgive me. It is just that . . . just that I miss them. I miss them so."

New tears came, but more gently now. At last he was able to ask, "How long, how long has it been?"

"The books say that Senusert III began his reign around 1878 B.C. That would be . . . eh, almost four thousand years ago."

"Four thousand," he whispered, and sank into shadowed thought. Everything he knew had been dead for four thousand years—everything except the duty that had sent him here. He had no wish to live on without them, not in this frightful, alien world. But he must. Or their eternal life would end as well. He had abandoned them all during their lives, but he would not abandon them now in death. Ironic. He had spent most of his life trying to avoid duty. But he must fulfill this one.

Calm now, he looked up at the girl. Suddenly remembering another cause of his distress, he laughed shakily. "I guess this means it's been four thousand years since I have had anything to eat. Could I possibly . . ."

"Oh! Of course. How awful. Yes, the kitchen's this way."

She led him back down the hall and into another room, bright with sunshine and flowered curtains. She pointed to a chair and table, and he sat and watched her rummage about in a large white chest and several cupboards, finally bringing out a plate and an odd assortment of food.

Soon he had before him a loaf of already-sliced bread, a rectangle of butter, some unfamiliar-looking fruit, a hunk of cheese, and two clear glass jars, one filled with light brown stuff and one with red. The latter smelled enticing, but he didn't know quite what to do with it until she took two slices of bread for herself, slathered one with the red stuff and one with the brown, slapped them together, and started eating. Hungrily he followed her lead.

111

As they ate they talked, both fumbling to find ways to make themselves understood. He was gradually grasping her odd way of assembling his words, but she kept throwing in strange ones of her own.

"You do not know how good it is to find someone I can speak with. Are you the only Egyptian speaker in this whole city?"

"Nobody *speaks* Egyptian any more. A very few people read it. But you certainly pronounce things differently than we thought you would. I guess that's because you people didn't bother to write down your vowels. That is very annoying, you know."

"It's a waste of time if you know what the rest of the word is."

"That's the problem. We usually don't. But I guess you weren't counting on people who had never heard the language trying to read it four thousand years later."

He shook his head, pulling a long yellow fruit from a bowl and examining it curiously. "It seems there are many things we weren't counting on. And there is so much I need to know. This city is in Lower Egypt, isn't it? I saw no cliffs nearby."

"Yes, it's Cairo, the capital." He seemed unsure how to approach the fruit. "Here, let me help you. You have to open a banana by tearing the top like this."

He took a tentative bite, smiled approvingly, then lapsed into thought as he chewed. He started to ask one question, changed his mind, then posed another.

"Then this would be some distance from . . . where I was last. How did I get here?"

"My father and I found the tomb when we were digging another site—a Twelfth-Dynasty quarrymen's village."

"You are tomb robbers?"

"No, no! You don't have a word for it. We're students of history, I guess. Learning what we can about ancient Egypt by finding things people left."

He frowned, remembering the hoard of objects jammed in the other room. Whatever they called it, they were tomb robbers. In part, it was the effects of their work and that of all those before them that his mission was supposed to counteract. Still, she was his only link.

He phrased his next question cautiously. "There were a number of things placed with me. Are they all still here?"

"Most are. But some are on their way to England now."

"The urn I've been carrying, it was part of a pair. The other one, was it one of the things sent to this—wherever?"

"England. Yes, it was sent off just last night. The plane should have left just about the time the storm hit and thunder cracked the sarcophagus open. Oh. Are the two things related?"

He sighed. There was no point in hiding anything, not from the one person who might be able to give him some direction. "Yes, I was placed there to guard those two urns and prevent them from leaving Egypt—or if they did, to bring them back."

"You mean you were sealed away in a tomb all those years just to watch over a couple of old pots?"

Ameni smiled. Having eaten practically everything set before him, he felt considerably better. "That is just about what I said when they first explained it to me. Let me try explaining it to you."

When he had finished, Lorna felt shaken, shaken to the bones. She had been so thrilled over her discoveries, first at the quarry, then in the sarcophagus. But all she had really done was to meddle, to throw a glitch into some cosmic plan that was far, far above her. She had dragged this poor boy into a chaotic world four thousand years away from his own. What a complete mess she'd made of things.

She looked up to find the boy's large dark eyes studying her. "I am sorry," he said. "Here you have your own life in your own world, and suddenly I've thrust mine upon you."

She shook her head resolutely. The late afternoon sun slanting through the window turned her hair a tangled, fiery gold. "No, I've been the one to force my life and my world on you. Now I have to try to make up for it. If there is any way I can help, tell me. I will try."

TWELVE

The first thing he needed, Ameni realized, after quieting his hunger, was sleep. The sun was only now setting, but he had just passed the most exhausting night and day of his life. Lorna took him upstairs to her father's room. She pointed out the bed, explained how to switch the lights and ceiling fan on and off, then showed him the bathroom. She left him happily turning the faucets and flushing the toilet again and again. She imagined he would find that the twentieth century did offer a few advantages.

Once in her own room, Lorna lay in bed, sliding between wonder and worry. The worry was winning out. Should she tell her father about this? She had always considered herself pretty self-reliant. But suddenly she was feeling very small and inadequate.

The problem was, she wasn't sure how her father would react. She was certain he could be made to believe the truth of Ameni's story. But once he did, he'd probably become all ecstatic Egyptologist. Here would be a real-life ancient Egyptian, a king no less, right before him! Lorna was afraid her single-minded father would see Ameni only as an endless source of information, rather than as a lost kid burdened with an incredible task and very much in need of help.

No, she was afraid this problem was largely one of her own creating. Now she'd have to help solve it on her own.

The following morning, Lorna dressed quickly and hurried to the next room. She hesitated at the door, half-afraid and half-hoping that this business with living mummies was just some dream.

Quietly she opened the door and peered in. Someone was asleep in the bed. She tiptoed up to it. The person there had the black hair and olive skin of any Egyptian, but the face of one particular Egyptian whose four-thousand-year-old statue was in a room below. She shivered. He was sleeping here, in her apartment, no shriveled mummy but a real living person. And one with problems that were also very much alive.

They would have to keep his presence here a secret, at least until they figured out some plan. Fortunately Abdul Rahman's apartment was downstairs and at the front of the building. So if Ameni stayed up here, he should remain undetected. But she needed to tell him that.

It seemed a shame to wake him. She'd write a note. Walking quickly to her father's desk, she took out paper and pencil and wrote out a simple hieroglyphic message, giggling to herself. She had never written hieroglyphics for real, just for lessons or for fun, or to annoy people who couldn't read them. She wondered if her handwriting was as bad as her pronounciation.

Finally she left the note on a chair beside the bed, tiptoed out and downstairs. Abdul Rahman was already in the workroom. She walked in to find him staring at the open sarcophagus. Under his mustache, his mouth drooped in a confused frown. Lorna had her story well rehearsed.

"Isn't it wonderful!" she exclaimed theatrically. "It's a real sarcophagus after all. The lid was jolted loose during the storm. The inscription says it was made for a Kakure Amenemhat. But Dad must have been right about it's being a cenotaph. There was nothing inside but that cloth and a crook and flail."

Abdul Rahman was clearly impressed. He was young and enthusiastic, but his side of Egyptology was purely administrative. He ran the association's Cairo headquarters efficiently, but his grasp of hieroglyphics or other things academic was weak, and he tried to stay as far away as possible from the heat, dirt, and inconvenience of excavations.

For a while the two worked recording and packing up the remaining items. Lorna had replaced the urn among the other things. If they had to, they could probably get it back from the museum. But in the meantime, it would be safe in Egypt, and they couldn't afford any inquiry that its absence might bring.

After a time she excused herself, went into the kitchen and fixed an extra-large breakfast of fried eggs, toast, cornflakes, and orange juice. She piled it all on a tray and carried it upstairs.

Ameni was awake examining her father's books. He turned and smiled at her. "Your written language looks like this? It certainly is different. You write ours quite well, by the way."

"Thanks," she said putting the tray down on her father's desk. "Writing it is a lot easier than speaking it. I'm afraid I keep throwing in English words when I don't know the Egyptian."

Eagerly he joined her at breakfast. "I suppose I must try to learn both to read and to speak your language. That is, if that's what they use in the country where the urn's been sent." He watched for guidance as she poured cornflakes into a bowl and added milk from a pitcher.

"Yes, in England they speak English. They speak it some in Egypt too, but mostly it's Arabic here."

"How far away is England?"

Lorna jabbed a fork into her egg, loosing the yolk in a smooth yellow flood. She frowned, unsure how to convert miles into ancient Egyptian measurements. Instead she got up and brought a world globe over from its place on the bookshelf.

As she made room for it among the toast and marmalade, she noticed Ameni's look of total confusion. Not only had he never seen a globe, she realized, he had never even thought of a round earth. Sighing, she forged ahead.

"This is what the earth looks like. It's round like a ball."

"But . . ."

"No, don't argue, just accept it. In four thousand years, we have discovered a few things. Now this is Egypt here. See the Nile? And this is England, an island way up here."

He looked, his dark brows meeting in a puzzled frown. "I'm still not sure how far that is."

"Well, look closely at the Egypt part. Here's the Fayum. That's near the Twelfth-Dynasty capital of Itowe, right? And here's where we found you near a wadi that goes east from this bend of the river. So if you know how far those places are apart, you can get an idea how far Egypt is away from England."

His face quivered with dismay. "But that journey of mine took days and days. Traveling to England will take years!"

"Oh, we won't be taking a little sailboat. We'll fly."

His expression now bordered on fear. "You can fly?"

"Not by ourselves! We have machines that do it. I'll explain it all to you later, but I've got to get back down or Abdul Rahman will wonder what's become of me."

She stood up then and looked her companion over critically. "Not that you don't look terrific, but maybe you ought to wear something more . . . contemporary. Just in case someone sees you."

"Well, there's that thief's robe."

"Yuck! That's filthy. No, you're about my father's height, and he's got a lot of clothes here. Why don't you look around and find something you like. I'll be back in a while."

When she got down, Abdul Rahman was out, so she went into the library to try to find something that would give Ameni a better idea of places. She had just pulled out an atlas when she heard the Arab secretary returning.

"Miss Padgett," he called as he walked down the hall. "I have just received a telegram from your father. He said he is wrapping up the excavation for the season and will be back in town next Sunday. He also says that he trusts you got off to England all right."

Lorna blushed. "Yes, I'm sorry. I know I should have left

earlier, but there was so much to do here, and they aren't really expecting me at school at any particular time. But don't worry, you won't get blamed. I can still leave for England before Sunday, and he'll never be the wiser."

The other shook his head. "I should have arranged for your ticket as soon as you returned to Cairo. Should I go buy it now?"

"No! No, that's all right. I can do it. Daddy gave me the money. You just concentrate on getting these things off to the Cairo Museum so that will be accomplished by the time he gets back."

The young man still looked skeptical. Lorna frowned. "Don't worry. I'll go buy the ticket tomorrow."

"Shall I drive you?"

"No, I'll take a taxi. You have too much work here to have to babysit me."

"Well, perhaps . . ." He paused, looking out the window over her shoulder. "Miss Padgett, who is that?"

She followed his gaze and almost choked with horror. Ameni was walking in the garden wearing a bathrobe her father refused to wear. A horrible print some colleague had sent him as a joke from Hawaii. White splotched with turquoise and purple flowers.

"Oh that. Who's that? Oh, that's Ameni. . . . Dr. Ameni's son, that is. Surely you know Dr. Ameni, the eminent Egyptologist from . . . Malasia? They came by wanting to see the institute yesterday. His father's at some conference today, so the son came back. . . . just now, while you were out."

"Ah, well maybe I should go greet him on behalf of the association."

"No! No, there's no point. He only speaks Malay, you see.

No English, no Arabic. It's very awkward. He said, by sign language, he just wanted to see the garden. Now, about those things for the museum. Don't you think we should use that bubble-pack stuff?"

When Abdul Rahman finally finished his work and returned to his apartment, Lorna ran out into the garden. She found Ameni examining the garden hose. He had managed to get most of the bathrobe dripping wet, but he was fascinated with the device.

She didn't know which subject to broach first, then decided on the most critical. "Ameni, we have to leave soon."

He jumped up, looking ready to run.

"Not that soon. But within a week. We just got a message from my father. He's going to be back in Cairo next Sunday, and I need to have left for England by then."

"You are going to England?"

"Yes, I'm supposed to go to a wretched school there. The way I figure it, you can go with me when I leave. Daddy gave me enough money to buy a round-trip ticket. I'll just buy two one-ways instead."

She sat on a bench that had somehow avoided being sprayed by the hose. "There's only one problem. You don't have a passport."

Ameni frowned. She'd thrown a handful of new words at him, but only one seemed critical. "What is that, a passport?"

"It's an official paper that says you live in one country and lets you travel to others. You won't be able to leave Egypt without one."

"Then I must get one."

"Yeah, but that's not easy. You'd have to show your birth certificate, and probably sign a lot of things in Arabic. I know there are people about who make phoney passports. Spies and terrorists and such are always using them in thrillers. But I haven't any idea how to find them, and besides it's probably terribly expensive."

Lorna had been tossing in even more English, but still Ameni got the general drift. "Well, if I can't get one, or make one, I'll have to steal one."

"Steal a passport? Hmm. Maybe so, but where? My father's is with him, and besides, they have pictures in passports, and you don't look anything like him. I suppose I could try picking someone's pocket, but I'd probably get caught, and Abdul Rahman would have to bail me out of jail. Abdul Rahman! He's got a passport."

Their plans were quickly formed. Abdul Rahman usually went out in the evening. They'd wait until he'd left his apartment, then use a spare key and steal the passport.

"But from now on until we leave Cairo," Lorna concluded, "you'll have to stay out of his sight. He saw you here, and I had to pass you off as some visiting South-Seas type. I think we really need to find you something else to wear."

"You said to choose whatever I liked. The pattern is a little irregular. But it's quite colorful, don't you think? And it's very comfortable."

"Yes . . . but's it's not really what people wear out in public. Let's go up and see if we can find something else."

For a while that evening, Lorna thought Abdul Rahman was going to be difficult and not go out. He did almost every evening, at least to buy a newspaper. But generally he went to see a movie or sit in a coffeehouse with friends. This was a fine night to decide to be antisocial.

Lorna was about to quit lounging around the reception

room when she finally heard footsteps in the lobby and the front door open and close.

She sprinted upstairs. Soon Ameni was following her down again, dressed in a khaki shirt and blue jeans, with a belt cinching in the slightly large waist. Bundled under one arm were the ragged thief's robes. Even though the house was empty except for themselves, they both felt this sort of activity called for stealth. They tiptoed across the lobby to the front door.

Cautiously Ameni opened it and looked up and down the street. Then pulling the robe on over his clothes, he said, "All right, I am to lurk around like some street vagrant, and if I see him coming, I am to start whistling. Right?"

"Right," she said, twirling a key in her hand. "But this shouldn't take long if I can figure out where he keeps his papers. We should be finished well before he gets back."

Ameni felt both foolish and excited as he slipped outside and took up his post, lounging against a wall. Several people walked by from both directions, but none looked like the picture Lorna had shown him.

After a minute he glanced over his shoulder and was alarmed to see that the light Lorna had switched on could be seen under the curtains. Not blinding perhaps, but noticeable. He studied the street and decided to station himself further along at a place where the road bent, so he could see to give Lorna longer warning.

Nervously he waited at the corner, his glance swiveling between the street and the faintly lit window. She must be having trouble finding this thing they needed. Suddenly there was someone walking his way who looked rather like the man he was watching for. He stared, trying not to look as if he were staring. Then he was sure. Casually he strolled down the street whistling.

Only he realized he had gone too far. She would never hear his whistle. He looked back. Abdul Rahman was nearly up with him. He had to warn Lorna!

Quickly Ameni changed his stroll to a drunken stagger, threw back his head and began bellowing out that bawdy song he had heard from the drunk on the streets of Itowe. The song about a man coming home unexpectedly and finding a stranger in his bedroom.

Abdul Rahman shot him a disdainful glare and crossed to the other side of the street. Ameni swayed towards him and held out a hand, mumbling a plea for alms he'd heard often the day he wandered the streets of Cairo. Abdul Rahman dismissed him with a curt phrase and hurried on towards his home. Desperately Ameni staggered after him howling even louder the ancient Egyptian phrase about unexpected returns.

To his relief, the light beneath the curtain flicked out. Abdul Rahman, trying hard to ignore the rowdy drunk, was staring so hard at the pavement he did not notice. And when he came to the institute, he quickly climbed the stairs and let himself in.

The drunk instantly sobered but continued lounging about until light appeared again in the apartment window. He was just beginning to wonder how he himself would get back in when a window slid open at the other end of the building, and Lorna's coppery head appeared.

"Psst, Ameni, over here." He trotted over, and she whispered down at him. "Go around the building, and I'll let you in the back door. But tell me, is that the sort of thing they sang in Egyptian royal courts?"

Ameni laughed. "Not really. But experienced adventurers have to be ready for all emergencies."

Whistling the ancient tune, he walked around the house. Well, he thought, there was one duty he didn't have to bother with any more—protecting the dignity of the royal house.

THIRTEEN

The following day, Lorna took a taxi to the airline ticket office and bought two one-way tickets to London, one for herself and one for an Abdul Rahman residing in apartment two at the same address. She got them for Saturday, the last day before her father's scheduled return. That was cutting it tight, she knew, but she had a lot of preparing to do before leaving on this particular flight. And most of it revolved around her fellow passenger.

First there was the question of appearance. The picture in the passport was rather blurry and several years old. Ameni might pass for the subject if it were not for several features.

Both were slender and about the same height. But Abdul Rahman had a mustache and far less prominent ears.

Lorna raised the subject of the mustache first. "Of course, it's perfectly possible that you shaved it off after the picture was taken, but the more things seem the same on the surface, the less likely they are to look beneath. I don't suppose you can grow a mustache?"

"Give me a couple of years, and probably I can."

"Hmm. Well, maybe we can try a fake one. We can trim a little bit off your hair and glue it onto your lip." They experimented, and the result was so ludicrous it sent them both into hysterics. When Lorna finally recovered, she attempted to tackle the other problem.

"Well, never mind. You just decided to shave it off. But you know, perhaps if your hair were longer, the . . . eh, the difference in your ears wouldn't be so noticeable."

Ameni stiffened, then shrugged. "It's a family trait. Senusert, me, our father, grandfather, great-grandfather. The courtiers call them regal ears. I liked to think they were just being envious."

"Well, whatever, clearly Abdul Rahman is no descendent of your family. Still, his hair is a lot longer in this picture, and if yours were longer too it would sort of hide the ears."

"I can't grow that in a week either."

"True, but I have a wig."

"A black one?"

She blushed. "I've always hated this hair of mine—a bunch of rusty old wires. As a little kid, I bought a black wig at a jumble sale and used to pretend I was Lorna, Queen of the Nile." She blushed even deeper and hurried off to her room, calling, "I've still got it somewhere."

In a few minutes, she was back and plunked the wig on

Ameni's head while he sat in front of the mirror. It was much too long; the silky hair hung nearly to his waist.

"That's worse than the mustache," he snickered.

Undaunted, she rummaged in one of her father's drawers until she found a pair of fingernail scissors. She took a deep breath and began snipping at the long tresses. "Farewell to the fantasies of childhood," she sighed. "It always looked silly on me anyway, with my freckles and muddy green eyes."

"I think your eyes are a lovely color. And so is your hair. You mustn't be ashamed of it. Black hair is so ordinary, but yours is like the rising sun."

She blushed again and continued snipping.

The final product wasn't half bad. They kept checking it with the passport photo until the two looked very much alike. And the ears were subtly covered. Finally Ameni nodded his approval.

"If those border guards don't look too closely at this magic picture, I should be able to get through. But I won't be much use in England if I can't speak the language. We have a week though. Will you teach it to me?"

"Teach you English in a week? It'd take months, years!"

Ameni shook his bewigged head. "Ankhrekhu taught me all that Kushite, Syrian, and Hittite with the idea that if anyone ever invaded Egypt or stole the urn it would be one of them. He never imagined that history would sweep them . . . would sweep us all away." He was silent a moment. "But that training did give me a skill at languages. Let's get started."

Lorna dug around in boxes until she found some of the picture books she'd had as a little kid. They were useful but involved her in teaching more about things than their English names. Not only was Ameni unfamiliar with television, rockets, and clocks, he had never seen such baby-book standards as umbrellas, bears, and ice.

He grasped the alphabet very quickly though, and in a few days was working with some of the simpler books on his own. Lorna was relieved, since she had to spend a certain amount of time downstairs so Abdul Rahman would not get suspicious.

Whenever she could, however, she took part in the crash course. As they worked, she not only learned wonderful things about ancient Egypt, but she discovered she enjoyed the teaching. She had always thought that sort of people-helping job would be perfectly ghastly. Of course, a displaced Egyptian pharaoh was not your average pupil. Still it was far more fun than she'd imagined, helping someone who really needed help. And Lorna had to admit, Ameni was, as he said, an incredibly fast learner.

Friday afternoon he sat cross-legged on the bedroom floor studying "Bobby and Sally Go on Holiday." He had just finished "A Child's First Book of Bible Stories," which had required that Lorna give him a hasty, slightly muddled account of Christianity, Islam, and some of the world's other current religions. Now she was shuffling about trying to get the room back in order so her father would never guess it had had another tenant.

Suddenly someone knocked at the bedroom door. Abdul Rahman's muffled voice called, "Are you in there, Miss Padgett?"

She leaped to the door, passing Ameni as he dove under the bed. Slipping out of the narrowest crack possible, she closed it firmly behind her.

"What is it, Abdul Rahman? I said I could get the upstairs ready."

129

"I am sorry to bother you, Miss Padgett. But could you tell me please when your plane leaves tomorrow so I can plan my day."

"It leaves at one thirty-five in the afternoon, but you needn't make any plans around that. I can make sure I'm there in plenty of time."

"Oh, but I will drive you to the airport."

"Oh no! No, that's not necessary, I mean. I'll just take a taxi. You're far too busy, what with Daddy and the others coming back in two more days."

"But I must insist, Miss Padgett. Your father specifically instructed me to see that you got off to England safely. I was negligent in not seeing to it sooner, but at least I can personally see that you get to the plane all right."

"But Abdul Rahman . . ."

"No no. No arguments please, Miss Padgett. I know my duty to my employer. We will leave for the airport at eleven A.M."

Despairing, she watched him tromp officiously down the stairs. Then she slipped back into the room and peered under the bed. Two large dark eyes stared out at her.

"I understood enough of that to say we have a problem."

"We certainly do. We've got you a ticket and a passport, but how are we going to get you to the airport? You can hardly stow away in a suitcase."

"Is it too far to walk?"

"Much. I guess you'll just have to take a taxi by yourself. Do you think you can handle that?"

He had learned that a taxi was one of those self-running vehicles that had so terrified him. With no conviction at all, he said, "Yes, certainly. Just tell me what to do."

The following morning, feeling no more confident, Ameni

resolutely prepared for the trip. He got up early and dressed in jeans and T-shirt. He still thought trousers uncomfortable and barbaric, but Lorna insisted that men in England, and even many women, did not wear skirts.

Sitting in front of the mirror, he carefully put on the wig. He had no trouble with that. He'd had a trunk full of wigs for state occasions, not that he'd liked wearing them much. However, he still thought he should have a mustache. At their first ludicrous attempt, they'd simply trailed a wisp of hair over his upper lip. Now he thought he would try something more elaborate. He trimmed short bits off the bottom of the wig. Then he smeared a line of glue across his upper lip and started placing the hairs into it one by one with a pair of tweezers he'd found in a drawer. He frowned and cursed over the results as he went along, but was finally satisfied by the time Lorna checked in to see how he was doing.

She put down the breakfast she'd brought and looked at him with astonishment. "Is that part of being a god, growing a mustache overnight?"

"Inventiveness is also a divine trait. Does it look all right?"

"Perfect. What did you use? Rubber cement?"

He scowled at the bottle. "I think that's what this says."

"Phew. It must really stink, being under your nose like that."

"It does, and it itches."

"Well, don't sneeze. I've got to go down, it's almost time to leave. Now, you're sure you can handle your part?"

"Certainly. When I hear you drive away, I go downstairs, walk out, head up to the corner, and hail a taxi. Then I say 'airport please.' I've got the money you gave me here." He patted a jeans pocket.

She smiled. "You certainly look a lot more like a modern

Egyptian than when I first saw you. You'll do fine. I'll see you at the airline counter. 'Bye."

She left the room, and as he munched his egg sandwiches, Ameni wondered if she felt as confident as she sounded. He knew he didn't. He waited in the bedroom, his stomach tightening nervously around his breakfast, until he heard the kitchen door slam and a car start up and rumble out of the alley. Then he picked up the suitcase packed with a few of Dr. Padgett's clothes and resolutely headed downstairs.

His courage held until he reached the corner and faced the crazy flow of traffic. He let several taxis rush past him before he finally steeled himself to wave an arm and step out into the street. To his astonishment, the vehicle screeched to a halt. He fumbled with the door handle, finally opened it, and got into the back seat chanting loudly, "To the airport, please."

He was further astonished when the phrase worked and the driver immediately drove off in a new direction. Ameni leaned back and tried to enjoy the adventure.

That proved difficult. Everything passing by was so incredibly strange he felt again the rising wave of the panic he'd known that first day. He fought it down, making himself remember the reason for his being here. In the last week he had tried not to think much of that, instead submerging himself in learning the new language. Whenever his thoughts strayed to the past, he became unbearably homesick—for a home he could never see again. The adventures he had once dreamed of had not been like this. Even Sinuhe and the Shipwrecked Sailor eventually returned home. But where was his home in this alien world? Trying to keep his hand steady, he reached for the comforting lump of his amulet under the T-shirt.

The road to the airport had now cleared the busiest part

of town. His eyes widened at the sight of several large ungainly animals being led along it. Lorna had said they were called camels and were common beasts of burden in Egypt now. He was glad they hadn't been earlier. He couldn't imagine a god with a camel's head.

He smiled faintly. The gods. Yes, that was his problem. All his life he had asked the gods for adventures. But at the time, he had not known he was one of them and would be taken so seriously. And now he had to take the consequences seriously. He had to find that urn and return it. And then? The priests had never said anything about that. He could only hope that somehow the gods would guide him, and in the end give him a home with them. He certainly could have no home here.

The taxi pulled up to the the airport terminal, and panic hit him again. The place was as busy as an anthill, crawling with hurrying foreigners who all seemed to know where they were going. The air roared and shook with noise. He got out, almost forgetting to give the driver any money until a volley of incomprehensible Arabic reminded him to hand over a wad of bills. Then he hoisted his bag and walked toward the door Lorna had described.

Lorna. The gods had been with him there. Could anyone else in this alien world have been so right for him to meet? And now she was the only person who cared anything about him or his mission or offered him any hope of fulfilling it. Desperately he looked for her in the bustling crowd ahead.

Suddenly he saw her standing in a line. Smiling with relief, he hurried toward her, then stopped as he recognized the man beside her, the man whose face they had tried to copy on his own. Abruptly Ameni dropped into an empty seat, turning his head so Abdul Rahman would recognize neither himself, the strange boy from Malasia, nor the drunken street singer. He strained to hear their conversation, and even from under the wig his ears picked up Lorna's voice

"That's quite all right, Abdul Rahman. You really don't have to wait and put me on the plane. I can't get lost now."

"Ah but Miss, your father would want me to."

"My father would want you to be at the institute when he gets back. Suppose he comes a day early? He has been known to muddle dates, you know."

"Ah yes, that is true. Well, Miss Padgett, perhaps I should go. That is if you think you will be all right."

"Of course I will. Thank you for all your care. I'll be fine."

Abdul Rahman had no sooner left Lorna than a mustached boy looking vaguely like him slipped up beside her.

"Oh there you are. Thank God!" she whispered. "Quick, pop this in your mouth. Suck it, don't chew." She slipped him a large green lozenge which hesitantly he put in his mouth. His nose wrinkled.

"Yetch! This tastes awful."

"Hush! It's supposed to, and smell awful, too. Puff it about and cough a lot." She lowered her voice even further, almost sticking her face into his wig. "Once the passport people see you have an Egyptian passport, they'll probably talk to you in Arabic. But you've got a dreadful cold and have lost your voice. Now, start coughing, and do be careful of your mustache."

Immediately he threw himself into wracking, lung-wrenching coughs, spewing a medicinal cloud around them. Lorna hid a smile as people gradually inched away.

After he had repeated the performance several times, she whispered to him not to overdo it, or they'd quarantine him.

Then it was her turn to show her ticket and have her passport examined. The official glanced briefly at the document, looked up at her, and handed it back along with a boarding pass. "I trust you had a pleasant stay in Egypt, Miss Padgett," he said routinely as another man picked up her suitcase.

"Oh yes. My father's excavations have been very successful this year. I'll be back next winter. By the way, my father's assistant, Abdul Rahman, has a dreadful cold and has quite lost his voice. Please excuse him."

"Yes, yes," the man said, stepping back as Ameni and his noxious odor moved forward. "That happened to me last month. Very dreadful." Quickly he flipped through the passport, then handed it and the boarding pass to the boy who was currently convulsed in another cough.

"Next!"

The two were then directed to the passport-control desk where they went through the same performance, then down a corridor and through a metal detection gate, something Lorna was unable to explain satisfactorily in either Egyptian or English. When they finally found a couple of seats in the crowded, noisy waiting room, Ameni whispered urgently, "Can I spit this out now? It's foul."

"Not yet. The boarding-pass chap or the stewardess may toss some Arabic at you."

So Ameni continued to suck gloomily on the lozenge, throwing in an occasional cough and wishing he could scratch his unbearably itchy upper lip. Several small children chased each other noisily around the waiting room, ignoring the occasional hushing noises from their harassed mother. At last a pair of doors was thrown open, and everyone jumped up and began jostling toward them. The sun and heat hit brutally as they walked across the black pavement toward a set of stairs and a huge silver body, a bright mechanical bird with immovable wings.

Ameni balked at the foot of the stairs. "Are you sure this thing can fly?"

"Yes, go on. You're holding people up. I've flown on these lots of times."

In a bewildered daze, he mounted the stairs and, following the flight attendant's gesture, stumbled down the crowded aisle. When they reached the right row, Lorna pushed him toward the window seat, then rummaged in an overhead compartment and pulled out two thin blankets.

"You'll need these. I forgot to warn you about the air-conditioning. Here, let me help with the seatbelt."

Once strapped in, Ameni watched the activity outside his thick little window. Small trucks scooted around, and men waved their arms and shouted orders. In the distance, a great silver machine like their own rolled with rising speed and noise along the ground, then suddenly rose into the air. Beyond it, another angled down from the sky and repeated the process in reverse.

Then it was their turn. The engines on the wings roared into life, and the plane began vibrating and rumbling forward while uniformed people in the aisle tried to tell them about emergency procedures in various languages, none of which could be heard above the noise. As they rolled faster and faster along the runway, Ameni reached a hand to the lumpy amulet under his shirt. He was grateful when Lorna gripped his other hand.

"It's perfectly safe, really," she assured him again.

He smiled at her weakly, and when he turned back to the window, they were off the ground. The huge airport was already shrinking and dropping behind them, and soon the whole spreading city looked like a tiny clay model. He gasped at a brief glimpse of Giza and the Old Kingdom pyramids, ancient even to him. Then they swung around over the Nile and followed its braided course northward toward the wrinkled green waters of the Mediterranean.

"Well," Lorna said after a while, "what do you think of flying now?"

He smiled, shaking his head. "If I had known that becoming the Living Horus meant that some day I'd actually have a chance to fly like the god, I might not have objected as much."

For Lorna the flight was familiar and tedious, but her companion never tired of watching the sea and the billowy mountains of clouds passing below. Briefly he turned his attention to an odd tray of even odder food before returning to the window and the fields and towns now sliding beneath them. They stopped for several hours in Rome, while Lorna in their mixture of English and Egyptian tried to tell him about the world-conquering empire that had risen and fallen thousands of years after his own.

Despite himself, Ameni found that as they continued northward the monotonous motion of the plane and the droning buzz of voices in the cabin were lulling him to sleep. Eventually he stopped fighting it and curled up under his blanket.

Lorna tried to remain awake so she could restrain his repeated attempts to scratch off his mustache in his sleep. The crying baby behind her helped, though it seemed to have no effect on Ameni's sleep. She imagined the royal nursery had been full of such sounds. Once she woke him to point out the cold, awesome beauty of the moon-washed Alps below. He watched in wonder for a while, then drifted back to sleep.

With the glare of the rising sun in her eyes, Lorna herself awoke to find they were beginning their approach to London. Guiltily she looked at her soundly sleeping companion, but his mustache was only slightly askew. She felt a wave of affection for him. A king and a god, maybe, but also a lost, duty-burdened kid, who by some quirk of fate was dependent on her, Lorna Padgett. Of all unlikely people! It should have been someone older, someone with more knowledge of the world than she, a recluse with an unorthodox education and an ineptness at dealing with people. But somehow it *was* she, and she'd just have to do the best she could.

Gently she shook his shoulder. "That's England below. We'll be in London soon."

Sleepily he looked out at the rolling green countryside, dotted with trees and towns. "Do your rivers flood over all that? It's green for such a distance."

She suppressed a giggle. "English rivers don't flood, not annually like the Nile anyway. It's green because it's not as hot here, and it rains a lot. You'll see."

Landing, disembarking, going through customs, and collecting luggage, were all a confusing blur to Ameni, and he stuck close to Lorna. The people they pushed past spoke languages he had never heard, wore clothes he had never imagined, and were of races he had never known existed. Finally Lorna hustled him down an alarming set of stairs that moved on their own, and then she shoved their way into a roaring, speeding monster she called an underground train. Ameni was beginning to think it would have been less tiring and confusing to spend years walking to England.

The train rumbled and shook its way past crowded brick homes and green pocket-sized gardens. Then it dropped down and continued on through dark tunnels, stopping frequently to let people on and off. Finally Lorna yelled over the noise that the next stop was theirs. He gripped his bag and followed her out through the crowd and up another moving staircase onto a street.

The first thing Ameni noticed was gray: tall gray buildings, wet gray sky, shivery gray cold. And even in the open, the air smelled far from fresh. The noise and the number of people and vehicles swarming around them was alarming. His companion, however, seemed perfectly comfortable. Glad of her confident presence, he followed her down streets that were overwhelmingly more alien than any he'd discovered in Cairo.

"What we've got to find first," Lorna said, "is a bed-and-breakfast house where we can leave our bags and give you a chance to wash off that mustache. You're beginning to molt. Actually we're both so tired I think we should put off going to the institute until tomorrow. Then first thing in the morning, we can learn where they've got the urn and start figuring out how to get it back."

Ameni just nodded and trudged along the crowded gray sidewalk. Long-term planning was beyond him at the moment. He just wanted to stop traveling.

Eventually they found a bed-and-breakfast house with two rooms available on the top floor. They took turns bathing in the small room two flights down. Then they ate fish and chips from a greasy-smelling restaurant around the corner and, heads still buzzing with travel, went to bed early.

The next morning, with Ameni shorn of mustache and wig, they ate breakfast in the little downstairs dining room, then stepped out again into the streets of London. Lorna was now wearing jeans like his, and Ameni suddenly understood why the English wore such ridiculous clothing. It was cold here. Under his own short black hair, even his head was cold. The fog of the previous day had lifted, but the sun shed little of its familiar baking warmth. And Lorna had said this was the country's warm season.

Lorna looked at the Egyptian as he stood gazing dubiously around him, shivering even in two shirts and a windbreaker. "We'll have to see about getting you a jacket. But let's go to the institute first, it's not far. I know this part of town pretty well. My dad and I always stay around here when we're in London. But if you want to see Buckingham Palace or something, we'll have to get a map like any other tourist."

Ameni wasn't sure he wanted to see any palaces. He was seeing far more than he could absorb as it was. No, the sooner he got that urn, the better. Though what would happen after that led to a whole chain of thought he still refused to link into.

Lorna led them through a maze of streets until four met at a small fenced-in park. Buildings of brick and stone lined the sides of the square. Confidently she walked up to one of these. Ameni puzzled out the inscription on a bronze plaque by the door: London Institute of the Association of Egyptian Archaeology, Founded 1863.

At the front desk, Lorna asked to see Dr. Witherspoon. The young bespectacled woman shook her head. "I am afraid Dr. Witherspoon is terribly busy at the moment. Perhaps you can call back another day."

"No, I really need to see him today. Would you please tell him that Lorna Padgett is here."

With an annoyed nod, the woman got up and walked into another room. Moments later a tall man with thinning hair and a wispy gray beard fluttered out.

"My, my. Lorna, dear, how good to see you. Your father

mentioned you would be returning to school, but he neglected to say you would be stopping for a visit."

"No, well, I decided to stay in London a couple of extra days and show my friend . . . eh, Abdul, around. He's very interested in Egyptology and was particularly anxious to see the institute."

"How do you do, young man," he said, distractedly grabbing Ameni's hand and shaking it. "Happy to have you both, of course, but I'm afraid I won't be able to give you much of a tour. We're all at sixes and sevens over this business of the theft, you see."

"Theft?"

"That's right, of course you wouldn't know about it. A couple of nights ago someone broke in and stole a number of things from the museum room. Took some of the flashiest items, I'm afraid, ones that would do best on the market. Knew what they were doing, all right. The police suspect they're part of a gang that's been operating for several years stealing artifacts from collections and museums all round the country. It's a terrible thing, really, a terrible thing."

Lorna tried to look shocked and angry instead of panicky. "What about the things we just sent you—from the wadi site? Are they all right?"

"No, they aren't, and that's what makes things so much worse. We hadn't even unpacked them. And having read your father's reports, I was so anxious to. They were still in the crate right by the door the thieves used. They must have thrown the crate in at the last moment, sort of a pig in a poke, I guess. But what a loss for us!"

Lorna's voice was tense as a tightrope. "And the police haven't a clue as to where the things might have been taken?"

"None at all, though they suspect these thieves may have

booty stashed in several spots around the country. Some people will pay a lot for antiquities, you know, without inquiring too closely how the seller came by them. And your things will be harder to trace, never having been published or anything. This is so very very dreadful."

After more commiseration, the two young people left the building. Lorna walked across the street to the tree-filled park, scarcely daring to look at her companion. Finally she sat on a bench and stared down at her hands.

"This is awful, Ameni. I certainly didn't expect this."

The Egyptian slumped onto the bench beside her, shaking his head. "Maybe I did. When we walked up to the institute, I knew the urn wasn't there." He smashed a fist on the arm of the bench. "But what I don't know is where in this cold, gray country of yours it is!"

FOURTEEN

 Ameni and Lorna sat on the bench, staring at the path before them. They scarcely noticed the plump pigeons strutting up and down, pecking at suspected crumbs.

"So what happens now?" Lorna said.

"I don't know. I wasn't given any instructions really. Just charged with keeping those two urns safe and within Egypt. And so far I haven't done either. I wish . . ."

"Yes?"

"Well, it would be easier if somehow I could get in touch again. If there was somewhere I could go to reach them."

"Reach the gods? You mean like a church?"

"I don't know. In Cairo when I was in that building, the one you told me later was a Muslim mosque, I thought I felt them very faintly. But I don't think churches to other gods are really what I want. What I need is someplace . . . someplace more Egyptian."

"Hmm. Well, the institute certainly has a lot of Egyptian things, but it's so crowded I don't see how it could feel very holy. But . . . oh wait, I know. If there's one place in the world that feels as daunting as a church and has plenty of Egyptian artifacts, it's the British Museum."

"Is that anywhere near?"

"Sure, just a few blocks. Come on, it's worth a try anyway."

When they got there, Ameni found the massive gates, great plaza, and monumental columned facade certainly daunting enough. The style, though different from the temples he had known, had the same trick of impressing visitors with their own insignificance.

And inside, standing in the lobby at the foot of a grand marble staircase, Ameni felt daunted to the point of helplessness. But Lorna seemed at home.

"I imagine you'd like to look around some. There's enough stuff from different cultures here to keep you busy for weeks. But it's the Egyptian galleries we need first."

With Ameni close at her heels, she made her way through the busy gift shop, through a room full of Assyrian things, and finally turned into the Egyptian Sculpture Gallery. Ameni stopped dead.

In the tall, skylit hall stood statues and pillars, stelae, and chunks of buildings. Calmly Lorna moved among the crowds of tourists. "That's the Rosetta stone—see, it's got three scripts on it. Translating that is what made it possible to understand ancient Egyptian, so people like me could mispronounce it. Let's go to the Middle Kingdom section."

The jumble around them confused and oppressed Ameni. Nothing was in its proper context. Tomb stelae never meant to be seen by strangers were displayed next to boasting public monuments and sacred figures from secret shrines. He watched in horror as a schoolgirl dumped the contents of her purse onto the granite back of a sacred scarab and pawed around for a lipstick. Someone else put his arm around the statue of a priest and had his picture taken. Desecrators and vandals, Ameni thought, the lot of them.

Not noticing anything inappropriate, Lorna led him on toward the middle of the gallery. "This is mostly Twelfth-Dynasty stuff here."

She waved a hand around several groupings of statues. With a choked gasp, Ameni's eyes stopped at one. The granite head of a pharaoh, long ago broken from its monumental shoulders, rested on a stone pedestal. Senusert II, the father whose burial he had never seen, looked down at him across four thousand years.

Lorna looked from one face to the other and suddenly felt she was intruding. "I'll leave you here for a bit," she said softly. "There's something I want to pick up in the gift shop."

Ameni scarcely heard her. He turned at last from the time-battered head of the king to see three life-sized statues of his official successor, Senusert III. Slowly Ameni reached out a hand and touched the amulet carved into the stone of the king's chest. With his other hand, he touched its twin under his own shirt. His eyes misted, and he turned away.

Trying not to dissolve into tears, he forced himself to read label after label under the statues. One made him look up keenly at the stone face above. Large ears, strong chin, a tired frowning look to the face. Amenemhat III, son of his brother, a nephew and namesake he had never known.

Lorna found him standing before the statues of several Middle Kingdom nobles. "Look," he said pointing to one seated figure in flecked red stone. "Ankhrekhu, the one who got me into this. The sculptor certainly captured him. That's his lopsided smile, all right. As if one part of him was always happier than the other."

"He looks like a good man."

"He was, and a friend. Though if I could talk to him now, I might give him a piece of my mind." He sighed, and Lorna quickly brought out the booklet she had bought.

"This is something the museum people wrote about the Middle Kingdom: the Eleventh, Twelfth, and Thirteenth Dynasties. I thought you might want to know about some of the things that happened . . . later, I mean. Though there's probably a lot of stuff they don't know a thing about."

He was silent a moment. "What do they say about my brother?"

"Lots. He was probably the most important king of the Twelfth Dynasty. Early in his reign he built a canal around the rocks of the first cataract so he could secure Nubia."

"Oh, so he did that! We used to dig that canal in the garden. He was always talking about it."

She looked down at the book, trying to keep cool and businesslike. "Then later he invaded Syria. This says he was the first king actually to lead his army out of the Nile Valley."

Ameni smiled. So his brother too had gone off adventuring like Sinuhe. His statues made him look so burdened with duty, it had appeared he might never have done anything he really enjoyed.

Slowly Ameni walked down the gallery, not really wanting to see the monuments to later kings who had died a thousand years after his own birth. He spoke to Lorna at his side. "Does it say anything about Senusert's family?"

She flipped a page. "Well, his Great Wife was someone named Merseger." She looked up in surprise at her companion's wry laugh.

"Poor Senusert. He knew that match was inevitable, but he never gave up hope that a crocodile might gobble her up in time to save him."

"I take it she was a dud."

"An officious, obnoxious, bossy bore. Does it mention any other wives?"

"Hmmm. Yes. This Merseger person was buried someplace else, but there was at least one queen's pyramid near Senusert's own. Someone named Neferhent."

A sharp intake of breath. Lorna looked at his face and wished that whatever this meant, she had not said it. "I . . . I'm sorry."

"No. No, don't be. As far as they knew, I had died. I'm glad they had each other. They must have been happy."

Lorna wanted to cry, and she hardly knew the reason. Always names like this had been just names. Their relationships and accomplishments were things to puzzle out, to fit together like pieces of a great academic puzzle. She had never really thought of them as people who liked or disliked each other, who grieved at another's death, or planned and hoped for the future. She closed the book, slipping it into her purse.

"Maybe we should go upstairs. The Egyptian galleries there have a lot more statues of gods and such."

Upstairs, she immediately knew she had made a mistake when they stepped into the mummy room. Ameni's expression, which had seemed far away, hardened into anger.

"These shouldn't be here."

"Yes, but people are interested in mummies."

"They have no business staring at them. These people's families scrimped to give them proper burials so their eternal lives would be assured. And then you come along and drag them away to be gawked at!"

Lorna felt like sinking into the floor. "I know. And put like that, it is wrong. But their being here allows others to study and learn. It helps make their whole way of life remembered—immortal. The only way we can learn about the past is by studying what little is left."

He gave a snort and walked into the next room. Miserably Lorna trailed after him. Looking around she groaned at the rows and rows of *shwabti*s, servant figures taken from tombs.

But Ameni took no notice of those and instead gravitated to the right where the cases were filled with small statues of gods. The figures were made of every material: gold and silver, ivory and wood, pottery and fragile blue faience. He found a bench hemmed about by glass cases and sat down alone facing rows of encased gods.

Brooding, he hardly noticed them. He shouldn't have lost his temper with Lorna. She hadn't done all this, and anyway her intentions, at least, were good. True, those people lying in the other room had had their tombs ruthlessly desecrated. But wasn't that his mission here, to secure the afterlife for all believers whose bodies and grave goods had been mistreated? He had to find that urn. He owed it to those lying in the other room, whom he had never met, just as he owed it to the friends and family he had left.

Yet how was he going to do it? This was a big country; Lorna had shown him a map. Without some inkling of where to start, he could spend several lifetimes looking for it. Well, his fellow gods had sent him on this quest, and he would do the best he could for them. But they must know more than he about all this. Surely they could give him some clue.

For the first time he really looked at the case in front of him. Many small figures of gods stood in incongruous rows. Still, he felt some presence there. A bronze statuette of Osiris was on one side. Ameni fixed his gaze on him, then closed his eyes. Quietly he murmured an invocation.

"Homage to thee, great Osiris, King of Eternity, Governor of the World, whose forms are manifold and whose existence is everlasting.

"I call upon you now in need, I your son, the Living Horus, Lord of Upper and Lower Egypt, Kakure Amenemhat, Living Forever. I have done your bidding, oh great god. Even now I seek that over which you placed me as guardian. But it has been stolen away, and there is none but yourself who can tell me where to seek it. I beseech your aid."

With lowered voice he chanted on and on, and it seemed that the air about him darkened and thickened as with smoke, and through it, the small figures before him flickered with life. A voice, or many voices, came to him faintly, as if on a distant dry wind.

"Greetings, Living Horus, Guardian of Eternity. Your devotion and your trials are known to us. But you alone of us can walk and work among men. Our power is with the mysteries of our world and the elements of yours. That which you seek you must find on your own."

Even as he half saw them, the ancient shadows began to fade.

"Wait! Can you give me no guidance in this foreign land?"

"Remember," came the dry, whispered reply, "you are the last of your gods and the last of your people. Awareness of both will lead you, and both wait on your quest, that eternity might be sealed. Seek what can be touched not only with your hand but with your heart and mind. We await you."

The shadows deepened suddenly into pure dark, and the echoing whispers faded into a babble of human voices. He felt someone sit beside him on the bench. "Ameni, the lights in the museum suddenly went out. I was watching you sitting here. I almost saw . . . almost heard . . . Ameni, did you do this?"

He squeezed her hand in the dark. "No, not exactly. But I guess some forces are stronger than others."

Suddenly the lights blazed on again, and around them worried, annoyed voices broke into cheers and self-conscious laughter.

In the restored light, Lorna looked at him closely. "But there was something here."

"Yes there was. But what it left me with, I don't quite understand." He closed his eyes a moment. "But I think I know one thing. I know where to go next."

"You know where the urn is?"

He sat quietly a minute then pointed. "There."

"In the next room?"

"No, much further. I have no idea how much further, but it is someplace in that direction."

"Great. Someplace northwest of here. There are a lot of someplaces northwest of London. Oh well, it's a start." She squeezed his hand and pulled him to his feet. "I knew you weren't going to admit defeat."

He smiled grimly. "Not now, I'm not. Even displaced pharaohs have an intense dislike for thieves." He looked at her awkwardly. "However, I admit, motives do make a difference. I should not class all archaeologists that way."

FIFTEEN

On their way back to their rooms, they made two stops. One was at a military surplus store to buy Ameni a jacket. The second was at the bank where Lorna and her father kept an account.

"You know, we had better find that urn of yours soon," Lorna observed. "After a while when I don't show up at school for tutoring, someone will get in touch with my dad. He set up this bank account so I could withdraw money on my own in case of an emergency. This qualifies, I suppose. But if he checks up and finds that both me and my money are missing, he's going to think I've been abducted by terrorists or something."

"No, only by a mad mummy."

"You've been reading horror comics!"

"You had a few in your room in Cairo."

"Mmm. Well, maybe if we're lucky, they'll have one of the old mummy movies on television tonight, and you'll get an even better idea of the kind of stereotype you're up against. All that mummies in movies ever do is stagger around in tattered bandages and strangle people."

"Think I'd be more effective that way?"

The television that evening showed no mummy movies, but after dinner at a nearby Chinese restaurant, the two did settle into the hotel's little sitting room to watch a Japanese monster movie. Ameni found the saga of huge lizards knocking down even huger cities fascinating enough. But since there'd been no TV in the Cairo apartment, the very idea of a box that told stories in pictures engrossed him. He would have watched it all night if the proprietess hadn't shooed them to their rooms around midnight.

The next morning after eating breakfast and paying their bill, they set off again with their suitcases. The night before, Ameni had half-heartedly suggested that he should go off on his own, letting Lorna get on with her own life. She had firmly rejected the idea and since then had been busily working out a plan.

"The next stop," she announced now, "is a car-rental outfit. I found one near here in the phone book."

"May I ask why we need such a place?"

"So we can rent a car and drive northwest."

"You can drive one of those things?"

"Well, no, not legally. I'm too young. But I know how to. My dad's let me drive the Landrover for years, and those things are a lot more complicated than the little toys they rent here."

"But won't they check how old you are?"

"Sure. That's why *you* are going to rent the car."

"Me! I haven't any idea how to make one of those things go."

"Oh, I'll do the driving, but you're the one with the driver's license."

"Huh?"

"Well, Abdul Rahman kept his international driver's license filed away with his passport. So I filched both just in case. His Egyptian driver's license is the one he uses every day, so he won't miss this one for a while."

An hour later the possessor of an international driver's license was slouched down in the passenger seat of a bright blue compact car. He was politely trying not to fling his hands over his eyes while the driver jerkily maneuvered their way through London traffic.

He did close his eyes as she delivered an ancient curse she'd just learned to a driver who honked at her for swerving into his lane.

"I have got to admit, driving in traffic's a little more complicated than in the desert. Too many cars fighting for the same space," she muttered. "But I'll get the hang of it."

Her passenger slumped further down into his seat, clutching his amulet and wondering which of his fellow gods was most appropriate to pray to.

"Once we get out of the city and onto a motorway, it will be a lot easier," she assured him. "But what would make it easier yet would be to have a better idea of where we're heading. What are you feeling at the moment?"

"Terror! No, sorry. I'll try." He sat up, closed his eyes, and tried to relax. Among all the sensations battering him, the one he sought was hard to pick out. But there was something there. A faint tie, a dependence, almost as if a cord were pulling gently from . . .

"There." He opened his eyes, pointing. "It's that direction."

"Right." She consulted a map crumpled out on the seat between them. "Well, if I can figure out how, I'll double back through this maze of lines and take the M40. I hope we don't have to go too far. We could keep going northwest until we reach the Isle of Skye."

As they left the city, the traffic did ease some, and Ameni began enjoying himself. "You know, it really is a beautiful country," he said after a while. "But . . ."

"But?"

"When I used to dream of going off and seeing foreign lands, I never dreamed lands came quite this foreign."

They continued along the M40 with Lorna occasionally asking if they were still on the right track and Ameni confirming that they were. After a couple of hours, Lorna said, "That sign says we're almost to Oxford. Is that where we're heading?"

"Is that the city over there?" Ameni asked, pointing to a pale skyline punctuated by spires.

"Should be."

He was silent a minute. "I don't know. It seems this is only good for direction, not closeness."

Lorna sighed. The thrill of driving in England was fast fading. Taking a deep breath, she drove on past an Oxford exit. A minute later Ameni swiveled around. "It's dropping behind us now. That city must be the place!"

"Eureka!" Lorna cried, to Ameni's bewilderment, and she flipped on the turn signal for the next exit. Then she frowned again. "But Oxford's rather a big city. Any idea where in Oxford?"

"Not really. I keep getting a jumbled feeling as if . . . well, as if it were with a lot of other things from Egypt."

"Hmm. Could mean another museum, I suppose. Dad and I spent a summer in Oxford while he was giving a seminar or something. I was pretty little then, but I do think there were a number of museums."

Outside of town they stopped at a gas station. For the first time in her life, Lorna wished she knew something about makeup so she could try looking a few years older. But no one questioned her age.

When paying the bill she asked, "Can you tell me please, if there are any museums in Oxford?"

"Oh yes, plenty," the attendant said confidently. "Can't exactly direct you to any, but we've got brochures in the back that we're supposed to hand out to tourists. I'll get you some."

A few minutes later they had parked away from the pumps and were studying the brochures. "Now let's see," Lorna said thumbing through them. "Here's 'Oxford, a City of Spires.' Not interested in spires. 'Stately Homes of Oxfordshire.' No. Ah, here we go. 'Oxford: A Guide to Major Points of Interest.' " She flipped through the pages. "Here's the Ashmolean Museum—sounds like a possibility. And I think there used to be another one with a weird-sounding name. Sure, this is it. The Pitt Rivers Museum. Let's go to the Ashmolean first. I can find it easier."

In a few minutes they were driving by the museum's iron gates. "What do you think?" Lorna asked. "I bet there are plenty of Egyptian things in there."

Ameni closed his eyes but felt no compelling tug. "No, that's not the place."

"Of course," she said as they drove on, "the urn could just be stored in a warehouse or someplace with a bunch of other stolen Egyptian artifacts. Come to think of it, that makes more sense than the museum idea. But let's check out the Pitt Rivers anyway."

She consulted the map, then eventually saw an elaborate Victorian building ahead. She turned to Ameni and realized he could scarcely remain in his seat.

"Yes, that's it. The urn's in there, all right," he said, his voice tense.

"Boy what a scandal. 'Noted Museum Deals in Stolen Antiquities.' Let's go in and see what we see."

Once they parked the car, Ameni took the lead in walking to the museum, but inside the arched stone doorway, he stopped in wonder and not a little fear. The central court rose to a vaulted glass ceiling supported by fluted metal columns. Suspended from the ceiling and rising from the floor were stuffed animals, skeletons and models of large mammals and prehistoric beasts. Ameni's throat felt suddenly dry.

"You mean," he whispered to Lorna, "that creature we saw on television crunching cities wasn't just made up? Those things are real?"

"No. Godzilla's just some moviemaker's nightmare. But dinosaurs like these did live a long time ago. I mean a *really* long time ago. Millions of years before your ancestors were even building huts along the Nile."

"And they don't live any more?"

"Certainly not."

"Ah." He felt better. Sobek the crocodile god and the hideous Devourer of Souls had been enough to terrorize his childhood—creatures that might eat you if you didn't go to bed on time. But these other creatures, they didn't bear thinking of even now.

Consulting a map of the museum, and walking between and under the monsters, Lorna led them to the back of the hall away from the natural history section. Then after passing through several doorways, they entered a room that was incredibly huge and incredibly cluttered. Glass cases crammed with objects divided the floor into narrow, irregular aisles and lined every wall. A large painted totem pole towered like a giant tree at one end of the hall, and the hall itself was circled with two more galleries on which the backs of other cases could be seen.

"This guide book says they group things here by subject and not by culture. So we can't just go to the Egyptian section."

"We don't need to," Ameni said pulling his attention from the fascinating things in the cases. "It's up, up high somewhere."

A narrow stairway led them to the second story gallery, but even there Ameni shook his head and climbed on. Finally on the top floor, he stepped out, looked briefly around, and pointed to a door in a partition that cut off part of the gallery.

"In there."

Lorna tried the door. "Locked"

"That section is off-limits to the public, Miss," said a voice behind her. She spun around to see an elderly uniformed guard. "Students and professors do research in there. There's a lot more you can see in these galleries though. Wonderful spears and axes and such. Not that there's much time left this afternoon. Almost closing time."

"Oh, yes. Well, thank you. I'm sure we'll be back." She headed back down the stairs. Ameni looked longingly at the closed door, then followed.

"What are we going to do?" he whispered when he caught up with her.

"We'll just have to come back tomorrow. There must be some way to get in there, but we haven't time now to 'case the joint' as they say."

At the foot of the stairs, Lorna followed a guard's directions to the ladies' room, and Ameni wandered back to the front desk where he looked with fascination and a touch of longing at the bright plastic dinosaurs for sale there. As soon as Lorna rejoined him, they were ushered out with the last of the visitors.

She hurried him away from the others, bubbling with obvious excitement. "I've got it!" she whispered.

"Got what? The urn? You couldn't have."

"No, no. An idea—how to get the urn. There's a window in the ladies' room that looks out on a skinny little alley between some buildings. The alley should be easy enough to find again—there's some turquoise-painted machinery in it. I left the window just barely unlatched, so if we come back tonight we should be able to crawl in, get your urn, and be away by morning."

"You certainly don't lack confidence. When do we start?"

"After it's good and dark. Let's get a little dinner first."

"Correction—let's get a lot of dinner. I'm starving."

She looked at him with a wry smile. "You know, Ameni,

I've never had a lot to do with kids my own age, particularly boys. But there's a stereotype that says teenage boys are always hungry. I'm beginning to think it's true.

"A universal truth that spans nations and centuries. And now that your wisdom has been multiplied, let's eat."

They did that, with meat pies and ginger beer at the Bear, a half-timbered inn that boasted it had been there since 1242. Lorna was impressed until she realized that for her companion, 1242 must seem nearly as far into what had been his future as her own time. "Old," she decided, was a relative term.

Afterward they waited for night to fall, wandering the narrow streets and alleys of Oxford. Ameni was impressed with the buildings in a detached sort of way, but when they came to the river flowing gently through town, he felt suddenly more at home.

Between the grassy willow-hung banks, people in shallow boats were poling their way among ducks and swans and under arching stone bridges. Closing his eyes, he could see the little reed boat he had once propelled, hear papyrus rustling in the hot breeze and feel the sweat on his bare back as he and Nisu moved through the swamps. He shivered, not from cold, but from loss.

The two found a bench along the riverbank and together watched the spires and trees slowly blend into a sky that shaded from delicate green into violet and then deep indigo. From many directions, bells rang through the cool evening air. When at last even the city lights could not hide the stars, they left their quiet refuge and headed back toward the museum.

"I'm surprised I'm not exhausted" Lorna said. "I ought to

be with all this walking, on top of driving from London. I'll confess, that really was a lot worse than I'd imagined."

"Well, if we survived that, I guess we can handle about anything," Ameni said more jauntily than he felt.

The museum building with its turrets and gargoyles looked a good deal more daunting in the dark. For Lorna it suggested an ogre's castle; for Ameni it was purely alien, and the more frightening because of it.

When Lorna led them around back, they discovered a warren of university buildings of varying styles, which over the years had crowded in together, forming a jumbled maze. The two would-be thieves worked their way into one alley after another, crawling over garbage cans and under air ducts. And one after another the routes proved dead ends that had to be retraced.

Finally they wedged themselves into what was no more than a crawl space between a new building and the old museum. It turned a corner and narrowed down even further. Lorna was about to turn back when she saw a piece of machinery whose tubing in the faint light appeared vaguely turquoise. Sucking in her breath, she inched her way further along and folded herself around another corner. She saw the window.

"This is it," she whispered to the struggling, muttering figure behind her. Finally reaching the window, she slid a finger along the metal frame, felt the slender crack, and pulled.

With a reluctant squeak, it opened outward. She stuck her head in. The room smelled of disinfectant and lavatory soap. Hoisting herself up, she wriggled through the narrow opening, followed moments later by Ameni, who landed on the tile floor with an annoyed grunt.

161

"That was worse than the maze my father's architect designed for the royal pyramid. Now I feel almost like a tomb robber myself."

"Just remember, this is a much better cause. Now, we've got to be quiet. There's bound to be a night watchman about."

Stealthily they stole out the door and down a long, low hallway with dark doors on each side. At the end, a short flight of stairs led them to the gallery of the main hall. Webbed light filtered through the high glass ceiling. In it, the skeletons and stuffed specimens seemed to crouch like silent, waiting predators.

Lorna turned down an aisle of stuffed mammals and cases filled with shadowy bird shapes. Suddenly from a door ahead came a beam of light and a buoyant, tuneless whistling. Night watchman.

Lorna's crouched figure suddenly vanished to one side. Like a startled hare, Ameni crowded to the other, pushing his way under the legs of something huge, hairy, and dead. He hoped it was dead.

Footsteps and whistling moving closer. He saw a carelessly sweeping light beam, shoes, and trousered legs. Without pausing, they passed along the worn stone floor. He stayed still, recalling hounds and hares, sunny mornings with the other children, finding hiding places in the familiar halls of his own warm home. All far, far away.

Lorna poked at him. He crawled out from under his stuffed protector to find her dark figure hunched on the floor beside him. Rising to a silent crouch, she continued scuttling up the aisle, and Ameni moved close behind. They passed through one door and another until they stood at the foot of the narrow stairs.

She was starting up when Ameni put a hand on her shoulder. "No," he whispered. "This afternoon I couldn't see any way over that barrier, not on that floor at least. But I've been thinking about another idea." Quickly he whispered his plan. Then stationing her to keep watch near the foot of the stairs, he threaded his way between the cases on the ground floor.

Finally he reached the base of the giant wooden totem pole. In the faint light from the high skylights, its stacked animal figures were eerily menacing.

Standing on a chair that he dragged under the first beaked creature, Ameni cupped his hands around the carving and pulled himself up. With trepidation, he wondered whose gods these were. Wordlessly he formed a prayer asking forgiveness—and assistance.

More by feel than by sight, he climbed up the rest of the pole, finding handholds in carved eyes, ears, and open mouths. At last he clung to the highest creature. Its multiple heads rested against the rail of the top gallery, the partitioned off section.

Pulling himself over to the rail, he edged along, toes barely finding purchase on the scant dusty molding. Cases backing on the railing blocked access to the area beyond. But ahead, after the corner turned inward, he saw a gap between two cases, a gap wide enough to crawl through. He inched nearer, then stopped. The gap showed up because there was a light beyond it—a moving light and voices.

Cautiously he edged nearer.

"Gerry, I don't get it," a man's voice whispered harshly. "Aren't these the things that were just brought in a couple of days ago? What's the problem? Has someone caught on about that professor here letting us use this place?"

"No, nothing like that. This is one of the best spots we've

got; be a shame to lose it. No one thinks to look for stolen artifacts among a museum's old study collection."

"Right, but you're evading my question. Why do we have to lug this stuff down again?"

"Mike, you're forgetting the pecking order. You do what you're told, and I do the telling."

"You sound like a bloody Tory."

"Hmph. Grab that end will you? I suppose it can't hurt to tell you. It's just a matter of supply and demand. His lordship's got a rush order for some Egyptian things, a very rich client apparently, and this stuff might fit the bill."

There was a sound of scuffing, then the Mike voice said, "Okay, I'll buy that for the stuff we took down on the first load. But this crate weighs a ton, and it's never even been opened. How do we know it's worth carrying down?"

"Hmmm. You've got a point. Maybe it's just full of soil samples or something. Better open it and check if it's worth the sweat."

The sound of rending wood and nails, then a soft whistle. "It's worth it, all right. Look at that gold!"

"The old clothing's not worth much, but this pot's not bad. Surprising how much these things fetch."

Through the gap between cases, Ameni glimpsed the urn glowing coolly in the beam of a flashlight. He could also see an array of Polynesian harpoons on a worktable in front of the cases. Not allowing another thought, he leaped between the cases, grabbed a wicked-looking harpoon, and landed on the floor before the startled men.

Coldly, in halting English he said, "The jewelry does not matter, but the urn is mine."

"Where'd this loony spring from?" exclaimed Mike, the thinner of the two.

"Don't know," his hefty companion replied. "But his lordship doesn't like competitors, even amateurs." He pulled a gun from his pocket. "A few old trinkets aren't worth getting killed for, boy."

Cocky fools, Ameni thought. *He* was the one who was armed. That metal club in the Gerry fellow's hand wasn't worth a thing. "No one need be killed if you just put down the urn and leave."

"Must be something pretty special," Mike said, "if he prefers it to gold." He spat on the alabaster and rubbed the spot. "It does shine up nice."

"Filthy desecrator!" Ameni lunged forward with the harpoon. The other man, staggering back, fired his gun.

Noise and burning pain sent Ameni spinning backward into a table covered with statuettes. In a pain-washed blur, he saw the men grab up the crate and vanish as he and the statuettes slowly toppled to the floor.

He fought unconsciousness. An ebony figure of Anubis lay beside him, its jackal ears plated with gold. "Anubis, guardian of the gods, help me . . . keep on."

Blood trickled down his arm onto the fallen statue as he struggled to his feet.

Below, Lorna had been listening anxiously for the night watchman, when a gunshot ripped the dusty silence. Guns! Ameni didn't know anything about guns! In a panic, Lorna raced up the stairs only to be thrust aside at the first landing by two fleeing men carrying a crate.

She had almost reached the now open partition when Ameni staggered out and grabbed her shoulder. "They've got it. We've got to catch them!"

"You're shot!"

But Ameni was already running down the stairs, and she

sped after him. They reached the bottom just as the watch-man burst into the gallery. He reeled back, obviously thinking it was they who had the gun. From around the corner, he began blowing frantically on a whistle. Its shrill peal followed them as, Ameni in the lead, they wound their way through cases toward a back door now open to the night. A brown van was just rumbling out of the alley.

Ameni pelted after it to the street, only to see it speed around a corner and out of sight. He slumped against a wall. "I almost had it."

"That's true in more ways than one. Ameni, you can't take risks like that with guns."

"Is that what that was?" he said dully.

"Weapons lesson later. We can't hang around and get thrown in jail for stealing that stuff."

Underscoring her point, a siren began wailing toward them through the night.

Ameni did not feel like running anymore, but Lorna almost dragged him along the sidewalk. She was propelling him across the street when a screaming police car suddenly turned the corner and brushed them with its headlights.

"Try to run!" she yelled, and Ameni caught some of her panic.

They ran down a sidewalk, shadowed from streetlights by trees and bordered by large expensive-looking homes. The police car screeched to a halt behind them.

"In here!" Lorna hissed and ducked through an open gate. They raced down a gravel drive then found themselves among the clipped bushes of a formal garden. Precious little cover here, Lorna thought. Then she spied a rhododendron bush at the far edge of the garden, drooping over one of the paths. Sprinting towards it, they rolled in among the mulch and dew-wet leaves to lie panting and listening like hunted animals.

"They turned in through one of these gates," a voice called. "This one I think."

Footsteps on gravel, suddenly skidding to a halt. "Look at that, will you. Talk about guard dogs."

"Nobody came in here with that thing on guard. You wouldn't think they'd allow dogs like that in a city."

Quickly retreating footsteps, followed by a high uncanny howl. Three times it rose into the shivering night.

SIXTEEN

For hours the two lay under the flower-hung bush, cold clinging to them like the damp earth. Lorna did what she could for Ameni's arm by wrapping it tightly with a scarf. Gradually the burning sank into a dull, throbbing pain.

Down the street near the museum, the night continued to be troubled by the rumble of cars, radio voices, and flashing lights. Lorna wondered if the police would spend all night examining the scene and questioning the watchman. But eventually the jarring sounds faded, leaving nothing but the garden stillness and the liquid calls of nightbirds.

Cramped, wet, and generally miserable, the two crawled from their hiding place. Skulking from shadow to shadow they crossed to the gravel drive. Fearfully, Lorna looked for a guard dog, but saw none. Ameni had not really expected one.

Skirting the museum block, they finally came to their car, innocently waiting where Lorna had parked it that afternoon. Quickly she let them in, then fumbled in the glove compartment for the first-aid kit the car booklet said was there.

"Roll up your sleeve," she said professionally. She did not feel professional. She had never, never wanted to be a nurse, which was worse even than being a teacher. But the sight of his blood made her more worried than sick. She tore open several packets of alcohol-soaked gauze and patted them on the bloody torn skin.

Ameni hissed with pain and tried not to pass out.

Finally Lorna stopped daubing and tried to sound professional again. "It's hard to see with just the streetlight. But it really doesn't look too bad. 'Just a flesh wound' as they say in the movies. I'll try to bandage it up."

The resulting construction of gauze and tape was not as neat as she would have liked, but it seemed to do the job.

"Now, let's get out of town," she said, settling herself into the driver's seat. "I don't think we should be anywhere near here come morning."

She turned on the motor and cautiously drove without lights for several blocks. Wrapped in a car blanket, Ameni already seemed asleep in the seat beside her. But after a while, he turned his head toward her and said, "Wrong way."

"Huh?"

"We want to be going that way." He pointed nearly behind them. "They've taken it that way. Southwest, I think."

"Southwest. All right, we'll head that way tomorrow, but right now we need some sleep."

They were already well out into the country, and at the first sign of a tree-shielded lane, she pulled off, drove a while, and turned off the motor. Ameni was already asleep. Lorna opened her door and stepped into the quiet night. Gently she pulled his legs up onto the driver's seat and rearranged his blanket. Moments after crawling into the back seat, she was asleep as well.

The dawn chorus woke her. Birds chirped from trees and hedgerows, being far too enthusiastic about the morning. From head to toe, Lorna felt cold, cramped, rumpled, and grimy, and she was sure she looked as bad as she felt. Combing fingers through her tangled red hair, she pulled out twigs and leaves left from their camp under the rhododendrons. Stiffly she sat up and peered over the front seat.

Ameni was curled up like a cat, the blanket slumped to the car floor. His rumpled shirt was splotched with blood, though none of it seemed fresh. His thin face was smudged with dirt, and his tousled black hair studded with twigs. Pharaohs of Egypt don't always look like stone gods, she thought softly.

"Breakfast time," the Egyptian said without opening his eyes.

"Oh, you faker! No breakfast for anyone until we're presentable enough to be seen in public."

"That would involve opening my eyes and moving, neither of which I intend to do."

"If you can take off your shirt without either, then fine. But come on. I probably ought to change the bandage."

Ameni cringed, but sat up and gingerly stripped off his shirt. Lorna climbed over to the front seat and began peeling away the bandages. "How does it feel?"

"It hurts. Particularly when you pull the little hairs on my arm."

"No, I mean the wound!"

"It aches, but not as bad as last night."

It did not look as bad either, though Lorna wasn't sure what she should be looking for. It wasn't all red or infected-looking anyway. She put on more alcohol, then a less-hurried, slightly neater-looking bandage. Finally wadding up the bloodied shirt, scarf, and bandages, she opened the car door to the chill morning air. Stepping out, she waded through dewy grass and Queen Anne's lace to a pond, tied a rock into the bundle, and threw it into the calm water. It plunked heavily, bubbled a moment, then sank amid glassy ripples.

"That's what people in books do to get rid of evidence. Good thing I read some things besides Egyptology."

Ameni had already sorted through his suitcase and pulled out another shirt. The jacket too was torn and bloody, but the morning was far too cold not to wear it. Lorna unpacked a fresh blouse for herself, and after a moment's indecision went off behind a tree to put it on. She knew ancient Egyptians weren't hung up about nakedness. But *she* wasn't an ancient Egyptian.

When she returned, Ameni was stamping his dew-wet tennis shoes on the ground. "Is it always this cold and wet in England?"

"No, it's usually colder and wetter. We're going to have to get you a new jacket, then you've got to learn to stay away from guys with guns. Are we still heading southwest?"

He nodded, pointing off over some trees. "I hope breakfast lies that way, too."

They stopped at the next small town for gas and groceries. By the time they were on their way again, Lorna's prophecy was proving true. It was colder and wetter. Rain drizzled from a dreary gray sky. They drove on southwest, eating and watching the rain-blurred landscape and the hypnotic sweep of the windshield wipers.

Lorna was feeling more confident now about driving, so she let her thoughts drift to other things besides just staying on the road. There really hadn't been much time for thinking, she realized, since they'd landed in London. And then she had thought they were near the end of the adventure. They'd get the urn from the institute and somehow things would be resolved. She hadn't counted on this wild quest across England.

Not that she regretted it. It was just so bizarre. All her life, she'd managed to avoid having any real friends. She'd done that to herself, she admitted, through her own combination of fear, pride, and deliberate oddness. Yet here she was, doing all this illegal craziness to help a four-thousand-year-old boy-pharaoh. And she was doing it because he needed her help and she wanted to give it. Bizarre—and wonderful, too.

They drove on through the rain. Ameni was still tired and his arm hurt, but at every doubtful intersection, he pointed the way. The strange tie to the urn was becoming so familiar now, he hardly need consider. As they continued, the rain began to lighten into a fine gray mist. Piercing into it, they could see a single pale spire rising from a sprawl of lesser buildings ahead.

"What's that?" Ameni asked. The spire seemed taller and more graceful than any obelisk he'd seen in a temple courtyard.

"Salisbury Cathedral, I think. Let's stop at Salisbury to stretch our legs and get you a new jacket. Maybe one of the flashy tourist type. 'I've Seen the Tallest Spire in Britain.' How about pale green and pink?" She cringed, remembering the bathrobe. Maybe that's exactly what he would like.

At the tourist shop, he did linger over something similar, but then decided that since they might need to do some more sneaking around at night, he should take a black jacket with the city arms of Salisbury blazoned in gold.

Back outside, Ameni stared in admiration at the cathedral. "Want to play tourist for a bit and go see it?" she suggested.

He nodded and started out before she'd even finished her sentence. It was beautiful, but different from the grand buildings he had known. Those impressed with their massiveness and their solid enduring majesty. This building seemed composed more of light than of stone and soared upward with such ethereal grace it scarcely seemed bound to the earth.

Inside, the sense of airy lightness was greater still. Pale sunlight shafted through the tall, clear windows. It cast pools of light on the worn stone floor and sent a misty glow high among the soaring arches of the ceiling. At one end of the great space, a boys' choir was rehearsing. Their high, clear voices seemed to rise and mingle with the light and the delicate stone traceries.

Ameni felt a calmness here, and a presence. The gods were near. He could not see them among the trappings of this other religion, but he could feel them. Silently he breathed a prayer for guidance.

Outside again, Lorna paused, trying to remember where she'd parked the car, then headed down one of the winding streets. Ameni looked with interest at the shop windows. In London he'd been too dazed to pay much attention to the odd goods displayed. And now he knew he ought not spend the time. But it was tempting.

Suddenly he stopped in front of one shop. "Look at that!" he said, pointing an accusing finger.

Lorna returned and looked into the cluttered antique-shop window. Between a molting fan and a pair of beaded shoes was an unpainted pottery jar with the head of a baboon sculpted onto the lid.

"You mean that canopic jar?"

"Yes. That came from some poor person's tomb. This store is selling that?"

Lorna felt uncomfortable. "A lot of antiquities get sold this way. They change hands so often no one knows where they came from. Ameni, don't glower at me like that. Archaeologists don't like the trade any more than you do. It's hard to learn anything from objects out of context."

"Why is trade allowed in these sacred things? This jar is only pottery, not even a precious metal."

"People like to look at them, I guess. They are beautiful. And besides, they're rare, so they cost a lot of money and people feel important owning them."

"That's what those thieves were doing then—stealing things for this sort of trade."

"Yeah, and don't think it's only Egyptian stuff. It comes from every country—even some from around here. There were a lot of Roman towns in this area. People dig up things and sell them, even though they're not supposed to. Come on, let's go."

Seething with indignation, Ameni tramped after her. He was about to bark out another comment when Lorna clamped a hand over his mouth and pulled him back around a corner.

"A policeman's looking at our car!" she whispered urgently. "They probably found out about Abdul Rahman's passport and driver's license and traced us to the rent-a-car place. What do we do now?"

"Drive away when he's not looking."

"Great. Two days' driving in England, and I get into a Hollywood car chase. We'll have to walk."

Cautiously Ameni peered around the corner. "Nobody's there now."

"Probably gone for reinforcements," she said, peeping out under his arm. "Oh," she said after a long moment. Stepping from behind the corner, she began to laugh.

"What is it?"

Lorna walked to the car and pulled a slip of paper from under the windshield wiper. "A parking ticket. I blocked a fire hydrant!"

Getting into the car, she laughed until she was weak. "Imagination in overdrive again. My dad's probably not even aware that I'm not in school. He assumes everything outside his little world of archaeology just keeps chugging on as planned, and he seldom bothers to check. Even so, we'd better get moving. Next time could be for real."

They put together a hasty lunch from their bag of groceries, then drove out of Salisbury, Ameni directing them west now and slightly north. After a while, the lunch started to seem inadequate, and Ameni dragged his attention from the green landscape to rummage around in the bag. He pulled out a plastic-wrapped package, tore it open, and had just bitten into a frosted cream-filled cake when he felt a sudden mental tug. "Rwld!" he exclaimed through a mouthful of cake.

"What was that?"

He swallowed. "Right! Turn right up here."

Just ahead, a narrow gravel lane struck off to the right. Lorna swerved onto it, spraying gravel, but after only fifty yards, they were stopped by a sturdy spike-topped fence emblazoned with signs reading Private, Trespassers Will Be Prosecuted and Beware of Guard Dogs.

Lorna switched off the engine, and they stepped out of the car. "Somehow, I don't feel welcome." Through the bars of the gate, they saw a wooded drive and glimpsed a large brick house on the crest of a hill.

Ameni gripped the bars in frustration. "It's in there, all right. But how are we going to get at it? This place looks a lot harder to break into than that museum."

Lorna shivered. "Guard dogs. Great big Alsatians with slathery fangs. I hate those things."

Ameni wasn't sure what kind of dog an Alsatian was, but he got the general picture. "Still, we've got to get in there somehow."

Lorna was pacing in front of the gate. "This doesn't look like just another temporary hideout. It's probably their headquarters." She stopped pacing and sat thoughtfully on the hood of the car. "So first we have to find out something about the place. Maybe it's a stately home, and we could join a once-a-week tour. Though, somehow, the owner doesn't strike me as the public-spirited sort."

Ameni snorted. He had just puzzled out another sign warning that the fence was electrified. He wasn't sure what that meant, but it didn't sound friendly.

"Well, you could eat again, couldn't you?" Lorna said as she jumped down from the hood and opened the car door. "The best place to learn about a house or its owners is a local pub. Wasn't there one in the village we just passed through?"

A few minutes later, they pulled up to the pub. Ameni stepped eagerly from the car and headed to one of the two doors. Lorna ran up to him, grabbing his arm. "Not that one."

"Why not?"

"That's the public bar. We're not old enough." She looked at him and laughed. "Not unless they count your extra four thousand years."

She steered him to the saloon bar door. "This way we won't have to fool with IDs. Really, there's probably no one looking for us yet. But we want to leave as small a trail as possible." She shook her head. "That sounds as if it came right out of a spy story."

The only other customers inside were a man and his wife playing darts. The proprietor was standing behind the bar, leisurely polishing glasses. He looked up as they entered. "Hello, kids. What can I get you?"

They walked to the bar and plunked themselves down on the high stools. "A couple of bags of salt and vinegar crisps," Lorna said, then glanced at Ameni. "Better make that four bags of crisps, and two ginger beers."

Moments later he slid their glasses and bags of potato chips over the counter. "You two from the excavation?"

"No," Lorna answered, then looked up. "What excavation?"

"Professor Birdsley's. Comes here every year to dig at that old Roman site up on the downs. Usually brings a bunch of students with him, so I thought you might be some of them."

Lorna tore open a packet and began crunching thoughtfully. Ameni had already started on his second pack.

"Hmm. What Professor Birdsley is that? Do you know his first name?"

"I do that. It's Mortimer. Like I say, he's come here for years. A decent friendly sort of chap too. Nothing eggheaded about him."

Lorna took an excited, much too large swig of ginger beer. The pungent bubbles tickled down the wrong way and sent her into an explosion of coughing. Ameni slapped her on the back, and the proprietor brought her a glass of water.

"Thanks," she gasped at last, wiping the tears away. She cleared her throat. "But about this excavation, is it around here?"

"Right up on the downs. The track to it cuts off just past the fork in the road here. They've got an enclosure, what they call an 'historically rich area,' sandwiched right in between the army land and Lord Blackburn's estate."

Lorna's voice was still uncertain, so Ameni spoke up in his oddly accented English. "That estate, is it the big brick house we saw west of here? We've been exploring around, you see."

"Well, you don't want to go exploring around Lord Blackburn's place. If there's one thing he doesn't care for, it's curiosity seekers, or people of any sort, as far as I can see. Since he inherited the place several years back, he's put up more barbed wire and electric fences than the army probably owns. And his guard dogs—they'd put the hound of the Baskervilles to shame, they would."

By now Lorna had recovered. "Ugh. Don't worry, we'll stay well clear of those. But this excavation sounds interesting. Maybe we'll drive up and take a look at it."

"Right. Why don't you? They like visitors. Been up a couple of times myself." A bell jangled in the adjacent barroom. "Excuse me. Got some customers, and the wife's off to the store."

When they were alone, Lorna turned to Ameni, lowering

her voice so the dart players couldn't hear. "Kakure Amenemhat, I have got a proposition for you. You've already had
to turn thief on this mission of yours. How would you like to
take a further step into degradation and become an archaeologist?"

SEVENTEEN

 Ameni was terrified. The rest of Lorna's scheme sounded all right, but this part was frightful. After staying the night in the village, she insisted that *he* be the one to drive up to the excavation.

"I don't really remember Professor Birdsley very well," she had said. "He was on a grand Egyptian tour and stopped by our excavation of a New Kingdom necropolis several years ago. A chunky guy with shaggy eyebrows, I think. But he might remember me, or at least how old I was, and think there's something funny about my driving a car."

Ameni had protested. "He'll think there's plenty funny about *me* driving, when he sees the way I do it."

"It's not all that hard. I'll get it started, and you just turn the wheel the way you want the front end of the car to go. It's simple."

Simple it wasn't. He was discovering that it took only a *little* wheel turning, barely thinking about turning, to make the whole car turn. His course to begin with was a trail of swerving zigzags that wound up the lane like a drunken snake. Sprigs of weeds and bushes that caught in the fenders were souvenirs of his progress. He thanked any god who would listen that there were no cliffs along this road.

His erratic course had smoothed out slightly by the time the track opened onto a field. Gratefully Ameni aimed the car toward a row of other parked cars, then fearing he'd run into them, he slammed the brakes on so hard they both nearly catapulted through the windshield.

"How do I make it stop working?" Ameni asked, once he had caught his breath.

"Turn the key to the left," she replied shakily. "No wait. Put it in park first. That lever. Here, let me."

She jiggled the gear shift then pointed to the key he was to turn. He fumbled with it a moment. The steady rumbling suddenly dropped into silence.

The two of them sighed with relief, looked at each other, and laughed. "Clearly," Lorna said, "driving is not an inborn divine trait."

She got out of the car, glad to feel steady ground under her feet again. "But you got us here—alive at least. Now let's go find the professor and act like eager students. It may take days to really check out the Blackburn defenses, and this could be the perfect base of operations. Staying here would make us a lot less conspicuous in the neighborhood."

Ameni only nodded as he looked to the tents at the far end of the field, where a heavyset man was clearly watching them. "I hope he doesn't have me arrested for reckless driving."

As they walked toward the man, Lorna noticed that the professor's bushy eyebrows were meeting in a distinct frown. Probably annoyed at having to show more tourists around his site. She knew the feeling.

She tried for an intelligent bubbly expression. "Professor Birdsley, I'm glad we found you. You probably don't remember me, but I'm Lorna Padgett, Dr. Winfield Padgett's daughter. You visited our excavation in Egypt several years ago."

His frown disappeared. "Padgett? Winfield Padgett's daughter! Of course I remember. Are you still being as much help to your father as you were?"

"When he's not sending me off to England to get a 'real education.' But I heard you were working here, and since my friend and I were in the area, we decided to drop by. Ameni here is an Egyptian student, but he'll be studying archaeology in this country for a while. I thought it would be nice if he could see how things are done here."

"Wonderful. This is just the place—lot's of mud and trowel work. I'm just heading up to the dig now. I'll show you around."

"That is very kind of you, Professor," Ameni said in his careful English.

The professor walked briskly toward a stile over a pasture fence. "I'm always happy to show off this place to folks who'll appreciate it. A nice little Romano-British farmstead. We've been digging here for five seasons and keep learning things."

"Sounds exciting," Lorna said, almost running to keep up with him. "Actually, Professor, I know you use a lot of student volunteers, and I was wondering if we could stay and help for a little."

"Certainly. There's always room for experienced hands. And since one of our number rushed off to have her appendix out and another decided he didn't like mud, we even have a couple of extra tents."

The narrow footpath rose higher and higher over the downs. A clean, fresh wind blew about them, rolling over the grass in silver waves and carrying the distant cries of rooks and bleating sheep.

Lorna looked about her and smiled. "I admit, I like Egyptian sun and sand best, but England can be very nice."

"Yes, it's beautiful up here," Birdsley said. "I can see why our Romans built where they did. Such a feeling of land and sky."

Lorna glanced at Ameni and saw that his appreciation of the landscape focused on a large brick mansion crowning the opposite ridge.

She cleared her throat. "I see that some people still choose this sort of spot. That's quite an impressive place over there."

"Yes, the Blackburn Manor. Been in the family for centuries, I understand. Even the army couldn't drive them off. The present Lord Blackburn's a real curmudgeon, though. Stay clear of his place if you don't care to be electrocuted by fences or torn apart by dogs. For that matter, stay clear of our other neighbors too, if you don't care to be a target for army weapons testing. Ah, here we are now."

On the crest of the hill, the turf had been peeled away in a grid. Down in the squares, people were working with trowels and whisk brooms. The professor introduced them all around and then put the two newcomers to work in a square with a plump blond girl named Susan and an even blonder boy named Calvin.

Professor Birdsley stood on the ridge of earth between their square and the next, and pointed out features. "The section from here over is the edge of a courtyard. Its surface is harder packed and darker than the later, windblown material. In this corner we have a shrine, probably dedicated to Vesta or some local spring goddess. That black patch there is the ash dump from the blacksmith's forge."

Ameni had stepped up beside the professor and was trying to see the picture as he described it. Slowly the grid of meaningless dirt became the traces of someone's home, the yard where the children had played, the shed where the family had worked, the shrine where they had worshiped. That dark smudge was where an old well had gone dry and been filled in with kitchen trash. Ameni was impressed. It was almost as if the mysteries of some cult were unfolding before him.

As the morning work progressed, Ameni took surprising pleasure in learning to distinguish the different soils by their feel under his trowel or from hearing the exciting click as he encountered a hard red potsherd, a corroded nail, or a long lost coin in the dirt. Lunch was welcome and plentiful, but afterward he was not disappointed when they returned to the digging.

There was a certain satisfaction in exposing walls to sunlight that had been hidden for centuries. And the bantering conversation back and forth between the workers showed that they all shared this enthusiasm. Perhaps, he decided, he had been overly hasty in judging archaeologists. There was surely little value in the broken objects they were discovering, yet their work was granting a certain immortality to people whose whole way of life had been dead and forgotten for two thousand years. He really ought to apologize to Lorna.

As the golden afternoon wore on, the peace of the hillside was broken by an occasional distant boom. Ameni kept scanning the high blue sky, yet saw no clouds heralding a storm. Finally he asked about it, and blond Calvin provided the answer.

"Artillery practice. All beyond that fence is military land." He pointed to a faint silver thread that trailed over the downs, disappearing in the distance to the east, and to the west running up against the Blackburn estate. "They've been using that land for years, testing things—shells and mines and top-secret stuff, I imagine. The place must be riddled with craters."

"And with hazards," Professor Birdsley added as he walked up. "A chap down at the pub says he has a cousin whose legs were blown off when he went poaching on the other side of that fence and stepped on an unexploded mine. The antiquities people assured me that this part of the downs was never used for testing, even before it was fenced off. I trust they're right."

"What!" Susan exclaimed. "You don't want to uncover any ancient Roman bombs?"

Ameni did not really understand much of what they had been talking about and didn't want to expose his odd ignorance by asking. He knew these people had frightful weapons—the gun at Oxford had proven that. But whatever the details, the whole matter threw another complication into their plans. Half of the Blackburn estate was surrounded by this apparently dangerous army land.

After dinner in one of the camp's large wooden sheds,

Birdsley showed Lorna and Ameni the two small red tents they could use. But it was still light, and instead of retiring or joining the others in registering finds, the two set out for a walk.

Very deliberately they paced partway around the Blackburn fence but could find no weak spot. They did, however, get a better view of the house.

"Look at that place!" Lorna exclaimed from one vantage point. "Four stories, three wings, all those gables and chimneys—it's probably been added to for centuries. What a pile."

Ameni was focusing in on something more specific. "Take a look at the east wing over there. Do the windows look barred to you?"

She squinted through the fence. "Yes. Yes they do. Do you think that's where they stash their booty?"

"Could be. And look! Isn't that the brown van parked down there?"

"You're right. It is. I hope that doesn't mean we have to deal with those two thugs again."

"We won't have to deal with anybody unless we can figure out a way to get in there. It's possible, I suppose, that the back part of the fence next to the army land is less well maintained. But it doesn't sound like we can get to that without having our legs blown off."

As the long summer twilight began to fade, a door in the house opened and a figure walked across a courtyard to a small outbuilding. He opened a door and a pack of dark shapes burst out, baying hollowly. Lorna shuddered and involuntarily clutched Ameni's arm.

"The guard dogs. This fence isn't going to be our only problem. Let's go back."

Slowly they walked back to the camp. The booming they had heard all day continued, only now it was accompanied by flashes of light, which silhouetted the neighboring downs like distant heat lightning. Lorna wondered just how much Ameni had understood of the discussion this afternoon. She didn't really want to talk with him about modern weapons. The ancient Egyptians had been warlike at times, but they hadn't come up with the stupidity of atomic bombs.

The next morning they returned to the dig on the hill. Ameni began with a gnawing guilt that he wasn't more annoyed at the delay. But he soon forgot even that in the interest of the day's work. They were uncovering the remains of the shrine now, and kept coming across little figures of clay or metal in the shapes of people, or of arms, legs, or ears. And several were of domestic animals. Professor Birdsley explained that these were offerings to the goddess of the shrine begging her to heal those parts of the worshiper's body or to cure a sick animal or child. As he fingered them, Ameni thought about the old woman and her prayer on a scrap of broken pot that she'd offered to the god Sobek. People were not so different. Nor were their gods.

He frowned. Perhaps he should not be thinking like that. He had been sent by one set of gods to help one set of believers. Yet there was so much that was alike—in what people believed and in their places of worship. Even in this small broken shrine he could feel a presence of gods—his gods, and more.

He placed a hand on a worn stone. He had nothing to offer except a prayer. A prayer for guidance in doing what he must do.

Throughout the day, clouds built above them, high and

gray. In midafternoon they thickened then suddenly broke, drenching the diggers and sending them running down the hill, laughing and squealing with arms thrown over their heads. The rest of the afternoon was spent drying out around a small stove and singing various raucous songs.

Eventually the others asked Ameni for some Egyptian song. He tried to decline, but Lorna mischievously mentioned she'd heard him sing a very old, very bawdy song they might enjoy. After his blushing rendition, Lorna provided an only slightly censored translation, and he was both embarrassed and pleased to find himself the sudden center of laughing, approving attention.

Still, he was more relieved than usual at the call to dinner, even though several of the crew groaned at the revelation that it would be "bangers and mash." At a questioning look from him, Lorna explained, "That means sausages and mashed potatoes."

The trenches were far too wet for work the following morning, although sunlight was prying its way through the clouds. Professor Birdsley led them off instead to explore for a reputed Iron-Age site on another hill. Ameni, fidgeting with guilt and impatience, was whispering to Lorna that they should slip away for some exploration of their own, when something the professor was saying stopped him.

"It was reported in the twenties but hasn't been found since. No surface structures left, but I brought along a metal detector this year, so we should be able to pick up traces below the surface."

From out of a canvas bag he brought a pole with a box on one end and a flat metal disk on the other. "It works like this. You switch it on." He did so, and a faint humming filled the air. "And when the disk passes over buried metal, it squeals." He pulled a nail from his pocket, gouged a hole in the turf with his heel, then tromped the dirt back over the nail. Deliberately he passed the disk over the spot, and the hum rose to a high squeak.

"Well," the professor said, holding out the metal detector, "who wants to try first?"

Quickly Ameni stepped forward, but when actually handed the device, he held it as he would a snake. This was not as bad as the automobile, but all machines still struck him as creepy and unnatural.

Nevertheless, after renewed instructions from the ever-cheerful professor, Ameni set off walking slowly across the grass swinging the humming disk steadily back and forth. He hadn't gone far when a squeal stopped him, only to reveal a bottle cap woven into the roots of the grass. Another bleat a few feet further sent him scratching in the dirt to produce an old army button.

Some of the others lost interest and turned their attention to a mound of dirt beside a badger hole that the professor pointed out. Perhaps this small excavator had dug up some telltale potsherds.

Suddenly the detector in Ameni's hand squealed more loudly, and, ever hopeful, he pulled his trowel from a pocket and began probing in the dirt. The point struck something hard. Eagerly now he scraped away a larger hole, finally revealing a metal cylinder.

One of the remaining bystanders peered down at it. "Ah, just an old can. We've probably found an old army dump."

Refusing to be defeated, Ameni reached down and pried his find free. It was closed at both ends, and through the dirt he could make out writing. "It's got letters on it," he said, proud of his recently acquired ability to read them.

"Here's an *A*," He flicked away more dirt. "*T . . . O . . . M.*"

After a stunned pause, everyone in the circle stepped back. "Don't drop it!" somebody gasped.

Lorna went pale. She wished she'd talked to him about modern weapons after all. "Ameni, careful with that—it's dangerous. Like that gun in Oxford—worse even."

"Professor Birdsley," Susan shrieked, "we've dug up some sort of atom thing!" Birdsley left the badger hole at a run.

Meanwhile Ameni, unflustered, had continued rubbing dirt off the object. "I don't know what you're all so upset about. The stuff's not all *that* bad. It's probably too old to eat, though."

"Huh?" Calvin said, inching a little closer.

"Well, I've got the rest of the letters now—*P, O, T, A, T, O, M, A, S, H.* Isn't that what it says?"

The boy looked closer and chuckled with relief. "Good God, it does." Quickly he grabbed the cylinder from Ameni's hand and threw it toward Birdsley, who had just run up. "Here, Professor, an atomic grenade!"

The man yelped and jumped aside, then looked sheepishly from the innocent can to the students doubling up with laughter. Ameni just looked puzzled, and Lorna was laughing too hard to explain to him.

Finally Susan recovered enough to say, "Professor, I think you ought to give this boy a medal for valor or something. When we all thought that thing was a bomb, he didn't drop it or anything. He didn't even look scared."

"Good thing too," another hooted, "or it might have splattered potato mash all over us!"

190

Laughing in agreement and relief, everyone crowded around Ameni slapping him on the back and congratulating him for his courage. He still didn't understand about that can. But two other things were clear. These strange, alien people had accepted him into their lives. And now he had a tool with which he might fulfill his own life.

EIGHTEEN

That night there was more singing after dinner, but Ameni and Lorna retired to their tents early, hoping the others would do the same. At long last the camp quieted down, and the two of them slipped out again into the night. There was no distant gunnery practice. The silence was broken only by a few trilling insects, and the darkness thinned as a nearly full moon bathed the downs in a pale unreality.

Like moon-cast shadows, the two stole to the workshed, emerging moments later with a lumpy canvas bag. Silently they flitted over the silvered grass towards the army's long line of fencing.

This barrier was far less formidable than the one around the Blackburn estate. Several strands of barbed wire and occasional signs proclaiming Danger Area were considered sufficient to discourage intruders.

Still the wire was set closely enough to force the two to walk some distance along the fence until they found a spot where water had washed out a gully deep enough to let them crawl under the bottom strand.

As soon as he stood on the other side, Ameni looked at the ground as if it were paved with scorpions. Hastily he pulled out the metal detector and switched it on. Its low hum was reassuring. Swinging the detector before them like a magical wand, they cut across the army land to the point where the Blackburn fence jogged westward and out of sight.

They walked side by side, taking turns swinging the disk in slow, even arcs before them. The moon turned the grass to rippling silver, echoing the cool rippling call of a nightingale. But Lorna hardly noticed the beauty. Her mind was heavy with thoughts that had been growing all day.

"Ameni," she said at last, "what happens if we do find a way past the fence and to the house? What happens if you actually get hold of that urn?"

"And don't get killed in the process?" He was silent a minute, mechanically watching the sweep of the disk. "I suppose I will have to take it back to Egypt and hope the gods instruct me in what to do with it."

"And then what? What happens to you?"

Put into words, the thought made him flinch. He had scurried away from it often enough in his own mind. "I don't know. Presumably it will mean my exile is over. I . . . at first that was all I wanted, to complete my duty in this foreign world and join the gods and the others in theirs. But now . . ."

"But now what?"

"No. No, I suppose there really is no change. That world is the only place I belong. It's just that, well, yours no longer seems quite so strange and dreadful, for all that I don't belong to it."

"Oh, but you can, you do! Look at the folks on this dig, they like you, they've made a place for you. And they've only known you a few days. I . . . I've known you longer."

He smiled timidly for a moment, then his face hardened into a frown. "No, Lorna, it just won't do. I'm out of place here, four thousand years out of place. I can't deny that, as much as I might want to. Why, I don't even have a legal existence here. I had to steal someone else's papers just to be officially allowed to exist."

She was silent a minute. "That could be taken care of; I'm sure it could. We could talk to my father. I know that if anyone could be made to understand, he could." She was silent a minute. "I didn't tell him at first because I was afraid he might exploit you. I don't mean cruelly, but I was afraid he'd see you just as a source of information to be pumped. But now I think it really wouldn't be like that, not when he got to know you. He'd see you as a real person and a . . . a nice one, too.

"No, Ameni, I'm sure we could do something about getting you some legal identity. Then you could stay here or go back to Egypt with us. You could go to school, study things. It needn't be Egyptology, it could be law or astrophysics or something. You could have a whole future here! Would it really be so bad to go on living in this world?"

"No, I don't believe it would. But I was born to another world. I'm a god of a world whose gods are abandoned, a citizen of a world whose citizens are dust. If I belong anywhere, it's there."

Lorna had opened her mouth in further protest, when the detector gave a sudden sharp squeal. They stopped dead. Eyes wide, Ameni slowly moved the disk over the ground, tracing out the shape of the underground metal object. "It's huge," he whispered. "Maybe six feet long. Do they make bullets that big?"

"When they do, they're called bombs. Though this is probably just an old sheep trough. Still, let's go around."

After skirting the mysterious object, they moved on in silence. Neither wished to return to the earlier conversation. But its pain kept gnawing at both. Twice more the detector peeped, but each time for small objects that were easily avoided.

At last they reached the manor fence with its humming, bristling wire. To Lorna it looked like the wall of thorns in some fairy tale. She wondered if Ameni had grown up on stories like that. Fairy tales are not the usual sort of thing recorded on stone monuments. She hoped she got the chance to ask him. She had tried not to be too inquisitive, as she had feared her father might be. But there was so much she wanted to know still, about his people—and about him.

Slowly they walked along the fence. There were more weeds here, and one badger hole. But nothing that would allow them to crawl over or under. Then, halfway around, they came to the tree.

Just inside the fence stood an ancient hawthorn sagging under a mantle of white blossoms. It had stood there for generations, and the modern fence builders, not wanting to contest its right, had swerved around it. The lower branches had been cut back, but one of their higher fellows had recently cracked under age or wind. It now lay, bridgelike, across the top coil of barbed wire with its leafy twigs resting on the ground outside.

"This must have happened very recently," Ameni said looking at the barely wilted blossoms. "Maybe in that storm yesterday."

"Good thing," Lorna replied, "or Lord Blackburn would probably have had his gardeners clean it up by now. I hope they don't work nights."

Without another word, Ameni returned the magnetometer to its canvas bag and hid it among the weeds at the base of the fence. Then he turned to the branch. But Lorna was already scrambling up. He watched in admiration. There certainly were advantages to jeans and the other fashions of this world. He didn't regret wearing them now. But then, where he came from, princes usually didn't have to crawl up prickly hawthorn trees at night.

He followed her up, but was so anxious to avoid the electric wire he'd been warned about that he forgot the barbed wire and tore the sleeve of his jacket on the topmost strand. He hoped Lorna hadn't noticed. He didn't think she'd like having to buy a third jacket. When he landed beside her, however, she was trembling, her thoughts obviously on other things.

"Ameni, I've tried not to think of it up to now, but what about the dogs?"

"There really aren't that many of them, and this is a big

piece of land. We'll just have to keep quiet and hope they're on some other part of the estate, long enough to give us a chance to get to the house, anyway. It's not so very far. You can see one of the outbuildings through the trees there."

"Hmm, we couldn't see that one from the other side. What is it do you think? A chapel?"

"Don't know. But we ought to be able to see the main house from there."

"If we get that far. I know. I'm just being gloomy and stalling. Let's get started."

Crouching low to the ground, they crept from tree shadow to tree shadow, moving up the slope until the trees finally gave way and left them exposed on an open stretch of grass. Beyond it stood the building they'd glimpsed earlier. With its empty windows and broken tower, it was clearly a chapel long abandoned. But it was refuge.

Crouching even lower, they started toward it across the dew-sparkling grass. At a distance, something saw them and barked an alert. The two stopped a moment, then broke into a run. From the woods to their right came an answering cry, and a third rose from beyond the hill. They raced for the ruin as a dark shape streaked toward them over the pale grass. Behind them, a baying cry drew closer.

At last Ameni lurched through the broken stone window, seconds behind Lorna, and, he was sure, only seconds ahead of rending teeth.

"Over here!" Lorna cried in the darkness. "There're stairs!"

He stumbled after her, casting about for something to use as a weapon. But the building was only a shell—even the pews were gone. Well, if he had to die in this world, it was appropriate enough to do it in a holy place—even if it was holy to the wrong gods. Perhaps these gods couldn't help him, but maybe they could carry his regrets to his own gods.

He almost fell onto the stairs and was crawling up them when suddenly the window darkened. Moonlight silhouetted a huge dog shape and glinted silver in its eyes. The creature turned to its fellows and threw its head back to bay in triumph.

But the cry was not that of a dog. A shrill wail rose three times into the night, silencing the chirping insects. Then the creature was gone, running and yapping, a strange intruder drawing the other dogs in pursuit.

Ameni felt Lorna creep down to huddle shivering on the stair beside him. Grabbing her hand, he pulled her gently to her feet.

"We've been given our chance. We must make it through to the house—now."

The chapel doorway gaped open. He hated to leave the feeling of sanctuary. But he forced himself out, and with Lorna at his side sprinted over the open ground toward the dark bulk of the house.

Almost there, they threw themselves to the grass as a door opened and a flashlight beam swept over them. They heard two voices.

"They've got something this time."

"Yeah, but it sounds more like an animal than a person. Did you hear that cry?"

"Why do you think I brought my gun?"

Feet ran past. Moments later, two shadows rose from the grass and sped toward the house and the door that the others had left ajar. It was pitch black inside.

"Feels like a car in here," Lorna said in the darkness beside him. "And it smells oily. Must be a garage. Close the door and let's try to find a light switch. Then maybe we can get into the house without falling over the lawnmower or something."

Ameni knew about light switches by now. Carefully he felt over the walls, groping among saws and hammers that hung from assorted nails. Finally he felt what he wanted.

"Got it," he whispered, and pressed the switch.

With a noise like the end of the world, one wall of the garage began opening up. At the same time, a great bright light switched on overhead. The two men running far down the slope turned and gazed back in astonishment.

NINETEEN

"Automatic garage-door opener," Lorna moaned. "Just our luck."

Ameni wished he could vanish. Instead, he leaped for the now visible entrance to the house. "Inside, quick!"

He burst through the door and pounded down a long hallway, ignoring the doors on each side. Suddenly there was someone ahead of him blocking the hall.

He spun around, and over Lorna's head he saw two other figures just stepping through the far door. Trapped!

Desperately he tried a door beside him. Locked. But the

one opposite wasn't. He burst through and, dragging Lorna with him, rushed to the window. With a muffled squeal, Lorna was jerked away, just as a big arm tackled Ameni around the waist and brought him crashing down, overturning a table and smashing a lamp.

Still stunned, he was dragged to his feet and hustled stumbling down the corridor deeper into the house. Lorna, struggling and trying to kick her captor, was just ahead of him.

The burly man who held Ameni's arms laughed gruffly. "A lot of good those dogs are, chasing rabbits while a couple of kids just saunter into the house."

"No, the dogs were onto something, all right," said one of the others. "Maybe these kids had accomplices."

"If so, then these are the lucky ones," said the man still struggling with Lorna. "If you kick me one more time, brat, I won't take you to see his lordship. And he is so nice to visitors."

They found Lord Blackburn in the library, scanning a ledger and waiting for his lieutenants to report on the ruckus. An austere-looking gray-haired man, he raised an eyebrow in surprise as the pair was dragged in.

"A little young for business rivals, I think." He gestured toward two chairs, and the men thrust their captives into them. Lord Blackburn seated himself casually on the desk.

"Now children," he began calmly, "didn't you see the signs?"

They sat silently glaring down at the expensive oriental carpet.

"Look at me when I talk!" He stood up from the desk as two of the men grabbed the children's hair, jerking their heads up.

"That's better. Now I want to know why you were trespassing. It's not an easy thing to do around here, you know. You couldn't have just stumbled onto my property by mistake."

Again, no response.

"You will tell me why you are here!" He slammed a fist against the desk. Suddenly Ameni jumped up, eyes burning. "We are here because you stole something that is mine."

"Oh? Just *one* something? I thought when kids played amateur detective, they tried to solve all the world's crimes. Don't you want to impress Scotland Yard?"

"You are mere thieves, scum, below my notice. In time your own king will punish you as you deserve. My only concern is that urn—alabaster, Twelfth-Dynasty Egyptian. Give it to me, and we'll go."

"My God!" one of the other men exclaimed. "It's that same lunatic who jumped us in Oxford. Guess you didn't kill him, after all Gerry."

"Ah," Lord Blackburn said, standing up again. "That one? He does seem rather single-minded about that urn. Why is it so special, young man? It's pretty enough, but of no great value compared to other things."

"Other things," Ameni sneered, "like what's stored in the east wing of this place? That's trash, all of it. You've soiled it, despoiled it with your thieving hands. I thought it was the scholars who sullied those things, who robbed them of their meaning. But they take dead things and give them new life. You're no different from tomb robbers, ghouls. You rob, not to learn, but to fatten your purse and to give blasphemous strangers trinkets to gawk at!"

"I tell you," one of the men said, "this kid's a nut case."

Lord Blackburn ignored him. "Well, young man, it seems I and my occupation have not met with your approval. That crushes me, of course, but I still can not let you have that little vase. So sorry."

Suddenly Lorna spoke up. "You'd better watch your step, your lordship. Ever seen those old movies about the mummy's curse? They don't like to be thwarted, you know. Especially when something important is at stake. Give us the urn, and you can keep the rest."

"What are you talking about, child? Mummy's curses? Oh, come now. You'd be better off trying to frighten me with Sherlock Holmes."

"I used to think all that mummy stuff was bunk," she continued, defiantly," and most of it is. But if a pharaoh could bring down a curse on anyone, it would be on the likes of you. And his gods could do it. They aren't myths. I've learned that much."

"Where did these two come from?" the thin man asked.

"From out of a pharaoh's tomb, it seems," the large one entoned dramatically. "What do we do with them, your lordship? Shoot them or send them to the looney bin?"

Lord Blackburn strolled over to the window. "Both perfectly appropriate, it seems. But in this case it does need to look as if two children wandered onto private property and, regrettably, were attacked and killed by guard dogs. Use knives first, and let the dogs tidy things up."

Calmly he glanced out of the window. "Look at those clouds. Quite a storm coming. Well then, why don't you do the job in the back courtyard so the rain washes away any stains."

"But," Lorna screeched, "you can't just rub us out like in some gangster movie!"

Lord Blackburn turned towards her, a troubled frown on his face. "Correction. I *can*. The question is, should I? And unfortunately if you two know as much about our business as you seem to, then, mental defectives or not, you have to be disposed of." He gestured in dismissal. "I am sorry."

Abruptly Lorna and Ameni were dragged from the room, each with a guard holding their hands behind their backs and directing them roughly by the shoulder.

They stumbled down another corridor into a grand marble-floored hallway. Desperately Ameni looked around, then noticed an open door, one of several leading off the hall. He knew it to be his goal. In loud, clear ancient Egyptian he said, "That door on the right leads to the east wing. When I say so, bite his hand and run in there."

"Shut up, you foreign lunatic!" His guard shook him roughly and pushed him further across the hall.

"Now!"

Lorna swiveled and sunk her teeth into the hand at her shoulder. The man howled and briefly let go. She wrenched herself away and sped after Ameni, who was disappearing through the door while his own guard jumped about in pain.

The door led to a hall, another door, then a long dark room crowded with bulking shapes. She raced past what might have been buddhas and many-armed gods of Asia. It was hard to tell. The clouds Lord Blackburn had mentioned now shrouded the moon.

At the far end of the room was a narrow staircase. Unerringly Ameni ran toward it and started up. Lorna could hear running footsteps behind them now. She quickened her pace.

On the next floor, Ameni waited until she stood panting beside him. Then he grabbed up a lacquered Japanese chest and hurled it down the stairs, bowling over the men who had just started up. He turned and raced up two more flights of stairs.

The top floor was Egyptian, a fact confirmed by a brief flash of lightning through the curtainless windows. Everywhere stood stelae, coffins, and statues of animal-headed gods.

Darkness closed again with a rumble of thunder. Lorna helped Ameni drag a wooden mummy-case to the top of the stairs and shove it down. Waiting just long enough to see it jam sideways, they took off again. Their path twisted between carvings and cases until Ameni suddenly stopped at a table. In the dim light, Lorna could see several vague shapes and the graceful outline of a pale stone urn. Reverently Ameni picked it up.

Raising his head, he looked at the statues crowding around them. All his attention focused on one, and he dropped to his knees before it.

Lightning flashed closer now. In one flare, Lorna saw the statue. Osiris, wrapped in mummy bands and wearing the crown of Upper and Lower Egypt, held the crossed crook and flail over his chest.

From where he crouched, Ameni suddenly raised his voice, chanting in ancient Egyptian. "Homage to thee, Osiris, Lord of Eternity, whose forms are manifold, whose existence everlasting. I call upon you, I your son, the Living Horus, Lord of the Two Lands, Kakure Amenemhat, Living Forever.

"I hold that over which I was set through eternity to guard. But our enemies are upon us. I crave your guidance now and your protection."

Even as his voice lapsed into silence, Lorna could hear over the rumbling thunder the sound of footsteps running from another direction, from some staircase left unblocked. She shrank back among the looming statues. But Ameni seemed unaware of danger. His face, lit by repeated flashes of lightning, was turned in rapt attention to that of the god.

Slowly around him, silence seemed to spread, filling the room like a draft from a door suddenly blown open. The cold, waiting silence sealed out the crashing thunder, the angry yelling voices. Into it came movement, the half-seen movement of shadows. The statues around them seemed to melt and shiver with dark wavering life.

On the cold, sepulchral wind, the shadows moved around them, dimly seen figures that were human and animal and both. Heads of beasts and birds rode on human shoulders. The air filled with dry rustlings, with the clicking of claws and the scrape of sandaled feet, with the rasping of wings and beaks, and the dry snap of robes blown by a desert wind. A faint odor of incense hung about, and the stifling mustiness of long dead air.

Lorna scarcely dared look even at Ameni, but her eyes were drawn there. He kneeled at the feet of a crowned man whose burial wrappings wavered in and out of shadows. Beside him stood a woman of soft, dawnlike beauty, while the young man at her side had the fierce head of a hawk. At their feet crouched a huge black jackal, its muzzle and upright ears rimmed in golden light.

The crowned Lord of Eternity spoke one word, and the power and cold and dreadful waiting spread out to engulf the room. Four men crouched trembling behind a wooden crate, but there was no escape.

Slowly Ameni rose and walked towards the men. Lorna gasped at his lightning-lit face. It was the face of majesty and power she had seen carved in ancient stone. The urn he held and the amulet about his neck glowed with their own clear light.

"I, Kakure Amenemhat, asked from you that thing which the gods had given into my care so that eternity might endure.

You refused me and would have killed me and she who is my friend. Even as Osiris judges the hearts of the dead, so I, his son, call his judgment down upon you."

The four men moved back, incredulous stares shifting into terror. The boy advanced, and with him came the shadows, the half-seen shapes, visions from the walls of tombs. They moved forward until the men turned and, stumbling in panic, ran back through the room, their screams lost in the constant rumble and crash of thunder.

Suddenly the world became white brilliance and shattering sound. Lightning engulfed the house. Battered unconscious by light, sound, and fear, Lorna sank to the floor.

In time she recognized the hardness beneath her as that of dusty floorboards. She sat up. The shadowy power had left the room, and the seemingly endless peal of thunder no longer rang in her ears. It had been replaced by the dry crackle of flames.

"Ameni!" she called weakly. Around her the air was hot and acrid with smoke. "Ameni are you here?"

Footsteps came running toward her. "Yes, here!"

She turned, almost crying with relief. "I thought you had . . . gone with them."

"Couldn't leave you in this." Clutching the urn in one hand, he helped her to her feet, and they hurried between the now lifeless statues toward the staircase they had climbed earlier. But the smashed mummy case at its base was now ablaze.

As they retreated past the windows, Lorna glanced out. Over the broad sweep of lawn, several men were fleeing. A cloud of darkness and glimmering shapes flowed after them. Lorna laughed shakily. "If the police don't get them, the insane asylum will."

Ameni tugged at her arm. "There's another staircase this way."

The smoke was thickening as they ran back through the room, floorboards hot under their feet. Beyond was another room and another, crowded with crates and half-seen shapes. Finally they emerged onto a grand landing. Above, the ceiling was painted with cupids and rose vines, and from it hung a massive chandelier. Its crystals tinkled in the rising heat and glinted with reflected flame.

They hurried to the wide staircase and began running down. Above them, they could hear flames crackling on the roof and rafters groaning from the strain. Far below, the marble floor still seemed to be clear, though flames licked at its edges. They had reached the third-floor landing when a rending crack came from above.

With a sound like the fall of heaven, the crystal chandelier broke loose, pulling a chunk of flaming ceiling with it. The jangling, fiery horror smashed downward, tearing away part of the stairway as it went.

The two reeled back against the wall as half of the stairs crashed after the chandelier to the floor below.

Ameni grabbed at Lorna to keep her from toppling after, and the urn slipped from his grasp. Lorna twisted and lunged for it. She missed. It bounced down the stairs with her scrambling after it. Stretching desperately, she grasped its base.

"Got it!" she yelled. The edge of the stairs she stood on suddenly cracked and tilted sideways. She pitched over the edge, grabbing frantically at a piece of railing.

In moments Ameni was lying on the broken stairs. One hand jammed in a splintered crevice, he reached over with the other. Below him, Lorna swung from a severed banister, still clutching the urn in one hand. Seeing him, she reached it up toward him. "Here, take it! Quick!"

Her pale face and the stone urn both glowed red in the fiery light from below. He stretched out and closed his fingers around the rim of the urn.

Just then the railing Lorna clutched shrieked and jerked further away from the staircase. Ameni held the urn of eternal life in his hand. Beyond it hung his dying friend. With an anguished cry, he let loose the urn. It plummeted down, smashing on the flame-engulfed floor below. Stretching every muscle, he wrapped his fingers around Lorna's wrist just as the banister tore free and spiraled downward.

Painfully Ameni hauled her up until they huddled together on a broken landing. Clinging to him, Lorna realized he was sobbing and shaking as much as she. "Ameni. I didn't matter as much as the urn. Why did you do it?"

The question seemed to echo in a thousand voices, voices in the flames, in the cracking stone and scorching air. Around them, figures fluttered like shadows of flame. Human and not human, alike and not alike, shifting like facets of light, one and many.

The question repeated and grew in many voices and one. "Why, Kakure Amenemhat, did you choose as you did? Speak, so your heart can be weighed."

Ameni sat up. His face was set with neither defiance nor penitence, but with hopeless resignation. "I will speak, for my heart can not damn me more than my actions have already. My duty was to guard eternity. But surely it should need no guarding! Men and women win eternity by believing in the gods and guiding their lives by their gods' wishes. Is that not enough? The gods my people knew are forgotten, but others have taken their place, and other people live by their precepts—precepts much like ours. I worship you as Osiris, Lord of Eternity, whose forms are manifold and whose existence everlasting. Are your forms not indeed manifold? I have felt you in the shrines of other gods, and prayers left there have brought your aid.

"It must be life, not the trappings of death, that secures eternity. Surely people, whatever their gods, find eternity in their beliefs and actions in life. Stones sealed in a tomb are valueless next to one loyal, beloved life."

With a sob, Ameni crumpled to the floor. "I beg no forgiveness, father Osiris. Again, I have fled my duty."

The multiple voice sounded within the protective cocoon of flame. "No Living Horus, you have fulfilled it. Your priests understood imperfectly the flaws of their faith. We allowed them to set you aside, not that you might guard carven stone, but that you might seek the truth.

"And you have found it. Gods are one. Even as human needs give gods different forms, so it is the *lives* of people, not their rituals, that win their immortality. But also some awareness of that truth is needed. For unchanging centuries that was lacking. Only you, the last king and god of your people, only you could attain that for them. Only you could lay hold of the truth. And you have done so. For all your people now, eternity is secure."

The shapes and dry echoy voices thickened around him. "Your duty is fulfilled, Kakure Amenemhat. Would you join us now? Would you join us in eternity?" Flickering hands reached out toward him.

Ameni sat in silent, shaken turmoil. At last, voice scarcely audible, he said, "Can eternity wait one lifetime?"

Wavering shapes crackled and hissed, as if with laughter. "Eternity is everlasting. Life is man's duty within it."

Around them the flames fluttered, cooled, and faded away. Suddenly Ameni and Lorna were crouching alone on a charred and broken staircase. They were getting very wet. The storm clouds had broken open, and rain now fell in torrents. For several minutes while they had been encased in their illusion of flame, water had been pouring through the ragged gap in the ceiling to rise again in hissing steam from the floor below.

The flames that had threatened to consume the rooms of stolen antiquities had been reduced to damp, smoldering ashes. Now the air throbbed, not with heat, but with the steady drumming of rain.

Ameni stood up, a look of incredulous wonder slowly changing into joy. He grabbed Lorna's hands, and together they hurried down the ruined stairs.

Outside now, the rain was letting up. In the high distance, moonlight sliced through the tattered clouds. The wind was wet and fresh, already scouring away the smell of smoke and destruction. A few tentative insects had resumed chirping in the bushes.

Lorna took a deep breath, letting the clean new air surge through her. "The storm is over," she said simply.

"Yes. And I have been told to go and live the rest of a life." He hugged her exuberantly. "That is one duty I will gladly fulfill."

DATE DUE